HELEN GARNER

THE COLLECTED SHORT FICTION

STORIES

TEXT PUBLISHING
MELBOURNE AUSTRALIA

The Text Publishing Company
Swann House
22 William Street
Melbourne Victoria 3000
Australia
textpublishing.com.au

First published in Australia by The Text Publishing Company, 2017. Reprinted 2017.

The stories in this collection have been previously published in *My Hard Heart*, Penguin Books Australia, 1998, and *Postcards from Surfers*, McPhee Gribble Publishers, 1985.

Design by W. H. Chong.
Typeset by Midland Typesetting.

Printed and bound in Australia by Griffin Press, an Accredited ISO AS/NZS 14001:2004 Environmental Management System printer
The paper used in this book is manufactured only from wood grown in sustainable regrowth forests.

National Library of Australia Cataloguing-in-Publication
Creator: Garner, Helen, 1942– author.
Title: Stories : the collected short fiction / By Helen Garner.
ISBN: 9781925603095 (hardback)
ISBN: 9781925626179 (ebook)
Subjects: Short stories.
Australian fiction.

CONTENTS

A HAPPY STORY

I TURN FORTY-ONE. I buy the car. I drive it to the river-bank and park it under a tree. The sun is high and the grass on the river-bank is brown. It is the middle of the morning. I turn my back on the river and walk along the side of the Entertainment Centre until I find a door. I am the only person at the counter. The air inside is cool. The attendant has his feet up on a desk in the back room. He sees me, and comes out to serve me.

'Two tickets to Talking Heads,' I say.

He spins the seating plan round to face me. I look at it. I can't understand where the band will stand to play. I can't believe that the Entertainment Centre is not still full of water, is not still the Olympic Pool where, in 1956, Hungary played water polo against the USSR and people said there was blood in the water. What have they done with all the water? Pumped it out into the river that flows past two hundred yards away: let it run down to the sea.

I buy the tickets. They cost nearly twenty dollars each. I drive home the long way, in my car which is almost new.

I give the tickets to my kid. She crouches by the phone in her pointed shoes. Her friends are already going, are going to Simple Minds, are not allowed, have not got twenty dollars. It will have to be me.

'I can't *wait*,' says my kid every morning in her school uniform. The duty of going: I feel its weight. 'What will you wear?' she says.

I'm too old. I won't have the right clothes. It will start too late. The warm-up bands will be terrible. It'll hurt my ears. I'll get bored and spoil it for her. I'll get bored. I'll get bored. I'll get bored.

I sell my ticket to my sister. My daughter tries to be seemly about her exhilaration. My sister is a saxophone player. Her hair is fluffy, her arms are brown, she will bring honour upon my daughter in a public place.

She owns a tube of waxed cotton ear-plugs. She arrives, perfumed, slow-moving, with gracious smiles.

We stop for petrol. My daughter gets out too, as thin as a clothes peg in narrow black garments, and I show her how to use the dip-stick. My sister sits in the car laughing. 'You look so like each other,' she says, 'specially when you're doing something together and aren't aware of being watched.'

On Punt Road the car in front of us dawdles.

'Come on, fuckhead,' says my sister.

I accelerate with a smooth surge and change lanes.

'Helen!' says my sister beside me. 'I didn't know you were such a *reckless driver*!'

'She's not,' says my daughter from the back seat. 'She's only faking.'

My regret at having sold the ticket does not begin until I turn right off Punt Road into Swan Street and see the people walking along in groups towards the Entertainment Centre. They are happy. They are going to shout, to push past the bouncers and run down the front to dance. They are dressed up wonderfully, they almost skip as they walk. Shafts of light fire out from the old Olympic Pool into the darkening air. Men in white coats are waving the cars into the parking area.

'We'll get out here,' says my sister.

They kiss me goodbye, grinning, and scamper across the road. I do a U-turn and drive back to Punt Road. I shove in the first cassette my hand falls on. It is Elisabeth Schwarzkopf: she is singing a joyful song by Strauss. I do not understand the words but the chorus goes '*Habe Dank!*' The light is weird, there is a storminess, it is not yet dark enough for headlights. I try to sing like a soprano. My voice cracks, she sings too high for me, but as I fly up the little rise beside the Richmond football ground I say out loud, 'This is it. I am finally on the far side of the line.' *Habe Dank!*

POSTCARDS FROM
SURFERS

'One night I dreamed that I did not love, and
that night, released from all bonds, I lay as though
in a kind of soothing death.'
Colette

WE ARE DRIVING north from Coolangatta airport. Beside
the road the ocean heaves and heaves into waves which
do not break. The swells are dotted with boardriders in
black wet-suits, grim as sharks.

'Look at those idiots,' says my father.

'They must be freezing,' says my mother.

'But what about the principle of the wet-suit?' I say.
'Isn't there a thin layer of water between your skin and
the suit, and your body heat...'

'Could be,' says my father.

The road takes a sudden swing round a rocky

outcrop. Miles ahead of us, blurred in the milky air, I see a dream city: its cream, its silver, its turquoise towers thrust in a cluster from a distant spit.

'What—is that Brisbane?'

'No,' says my mother. 'That's Surfers.'

My father's car has a built-in computer. If he exceeds the speed limit, the dashboard emits a discreet but insistent pinging. Lights flash, and the pressure of his right foot lessens. He controls the windows from a panel between the two front seats. We cruise past a Valiant parked by the highway with a FOR SALE sign propped in its back window.

'Look at that,' says my mother. 'A WA number-plate. Probably thrashed it across the Nullarbor and now they reckon they'll flog it.'

'Pro'ly stolen,' says my father. 'See the sticker? ALL YOU VIRGINS, THANKS FOR NOTHING. You can just see what sort of a pin'ead he'd be. Brain the size of a pea.'

Close up, many of the turquoise towers are not yet sold. 'Every conceivable feature,' the signs say. They have names like Capricornia, Biarritz, The Breakers, Acapulco, Rio.

I had a Brazilian friend when I lived in Paris. He showed me a postcard, once, of Rio where he was born and brought up. The card bore an aerial shot of a splendid, curved tropical beach, fringed with palms, its sand pure as snow.

'Why don't you live in Brazil,' I said, 'if it's as beautiful as this?'

'Because,' said my friend, 'right behind that beach there is a huge military base.'

In my turn I showed him a postcard of my country. It was a reproduction of that Streeton painting called *The Land of the Golden Fleece* which in my homesickness I kept standing on the heater in my bedroom. He studied it carefully. At last he turned his currant-coloured eyes to me and said, '*Les arbres sont rouges?*' Are the trees red?

Several years later, six months ago, I was rummaging through a box of old postcards in a junk shop in Rathdowne Street. Among the photos of damp cottages in Galway, of Raj hotels crumbling in bicycle-thronged Colombo, of glassy Canadian lakes flawed by the wake of a single canoe, I found two cards that I bought for a dollar each. One was a picture of downtown Rio, in black and white. The other, crudely tinted, showed Geelong, the town where I was born. The photographer must have stood on the high grassy bank that overlooks the Eastern Beach. He lined up his shot through the never-flowing fountain with its quartet of concrete wading birds (storks? cranes? I never asked my father: they have long orange

11

beaks and each bird holds one leg bent, as if about to take a step); through the fountain and out over the curving wooden promenade, from which we dived all summer, unsupervised, into the flat water; and across the bay to the You Yangs, the double-humped, low, volcanic cones, the only disturbance in the great basalt plains that lie between Geelong and Melbourne. These two cards in the same box! And I find them! Imagine! '*Cher Rubens,*' I wrote. '*Je t'envoie ces deux cartes postales, de nos deux villes natales…*'

Auntie Lorna has gone for a walk on the beach. My mother unlocks the door and slides open the flywire screen. She goes out into the bright air to tell her friend of my arrival. The ocean is right in front of the unit, only a hundred and fifty yards away. How can people be so sure of the boundary between land and sea that they have the confidence to build houses on it? The white doorsteps of the ocean travel and travel.

'Twelve o'clock,' says my father.

'Getting on for lunchtime,' I say.

'Getting towards it. Specially with that nice cold corned beef sitting there, and fresh brown bread. Think I'll have to try some of that choko relish. Ever eaten a choko?'

'I wouldn't know a choko if I fell over it.'

'Nor would I.'

He selects a serrated knife from the magnetised holder on the kitchen wall and quickly and skilfully, at the bench, makes himself a thick sandwich. He works with powerful concentration: when the meat flaps off the slice of bread, he rounds it up with a large, dramatic scooping movement and a sympathetic grimace of the lower lip. He picks up the sandwich in two hands, raises it to his mouth and takes a large bite. While he chews he breathes heavily through his nose.

'Want to make yourself something?' he says with his mouth full.

I stand up. He pushes the loaf of bread towards me with the back of his hand. He puts the other half of his sandwich on a green bread and butter plate and carries it to the table. He sits with his elbows on the pine wood, his knees wide apart, his belly relaxing on to his thighs, his high-arched, long-boned feet planted on the tiled floor. He eats, and gazes out to sea. The noise of his eating fills the room.

My mother and Auntie Lorna come up from the beach. I stand inside the wall of glass and watch them stop at the tap to hose the sand off their feet before they cross the grass to the door. They are two old women: they have to keep one hand on the tap in order to balance on the left foot and wash the right. I see that they are two old women, and yet they are neither young nor old. They are my mother and Auntie Lorna, two institutions. They slide back the wire door, smiling.

'Don't tramp sand everywhere,' says my father from the table.

They take no notice. Auntie Lorna kisses me, and holds me at arms' length with her head on one side. My mother prepares food and we eat, looking out at the water.

'You've missed the coronary brigade,' says my father. 'They get out on the beach about nine in the morning. You can pick 'em. They swing their arms up really high when they walk.' He laughs, looking down.

'Do you go for a walk every day too?' I ask.

'Six point six kilometres,' says my father.

'Got a pedometer, have you?'

'I just nutted it out,' says my father. 'We walk as far as a big white building, down that way, then we turn round and come back. Six point six altogether, there and back.'

'I might come with you.'

'You can if you like,' he says. He picks up his plate and carries it to the sink. 'We go after breakfast. You've missed today's.'

He goes to the couch and opens the newspaper on the low coffee table. He reads with his glasses down his nose and his hands loosely linked between his spread knees. The women wash up.

'Is there a shop nearby?' I ask my mother. 'I have to get some tampons.'

'Caught short, are you?' she says. 'I think they sell them at the shopping centre, along Sunbrite Avenue there near the bowling club. Want me to come with you?'

'I can find it.'

'I never could use those things,' says my mother, lowering her voice and glancing across the room at my father. 'Hazel told me about a terrible thing that happened to her. For days she kept noticing this revolting smell that was…emanating from her. She washed and washed, and couldn't get rid of it. Finally she was about to go to the doctor, but first she got down and had a look with the mirror. She saw this bit of thread and pulled it. The thing was *green*. She must've forgotten to take it out—it'd been there for days and days and *days*.'

We laugh with the tea towels up to our mouths. My father, on the other side of the room, looks up from the paper with the bent smile of someone not sure what the others are laughing at. I am always surprised when my mother comes out with a word like 'emanating'. At home I have a book called *An Outline of English Verse* which my mother used in her matriculation year. In the margins

15

of *The Rape of the Lock* she has made notations: 'bathos; reminiscent of Virgil; parody of Homer'. Her handwriting in these pencilled jottings, made forty-five years ago, is exactly as it is today: this makes me suspect, when I am not with her, that she is a closet intellectual.

Once or twice, on my way from the unit to the shopping centre, I think to see roses along a fence and run to look, but I find them to be some scentless, fleshy flower. I fall back. Beside a patch of yellow grass, pretty trees in a row are bearing and dropping white blossom-like flowers, but they look wrong to me, I do not recognise them: the blossoms too large, the branches too flat. I am dizzy from the flight. In Melbourne it is still winter, everything is bare.

I buy the tampons and look for the postcards. There they are, displayed in a tall revolving rack. There is a great deal of blue. Closer, I find colour photos of white beaches, duneless, palmless, on which half-naked people lie on their backs with their knees raised. The frequency of this posture, at random through the crowd, makes me feel like laughing. Most of the cards have GREETINGS FROM THE GOLD COAST or BROADBEACH or SURFERS PARADISE embossed in gold in one corner: I search for pictures without words. Another card, in several slightly differing versions, shows a graceful, big-breasted young girl lying in a seductive pose against some rocks: she is wearing a bikini and her whole head is covered by one of those latex masks that are sold in trick shops, the ones you pull on as a bandit pulls on a stocking. The mask represents the hideous, raddled, grinning face of an old woman, a witch. I stare at this photo for a long time. Is it simple, or does it hide some more mysterious signs and symbols?

I buy twelve GREETINGS FROM cards with views, some aerial, some from the ground. They cost twenty-five cents each.

'Want the envelopes?' says the girl. She is dressed in a flowered garment which is drawn up between her thighs like a nappy.

'Yes please.' The envelopes are so covered with coloured maps, logos and drawings of Australian fauna that there is barely room to write an address, but something about them attracts me. I buy a packet of Licorice Chews and eat them all on the way home: I stuff them in two at a time: my mouth floods with saliva. There are no rubbish bins so I put the papers in my pocket. Now that I have spent money here, now that I have rubbish to dispose of, I am no longer a stranger. In Paris there used to be signs in the streets that said, '*Le commerce, c'est la vie de la ville.*' Any traveller knows this to be the truth.

The women are knitting. They murmur and murmur. What they say never requires an answer. My father sharpens a pencil stub with his pocket knife, and folds the paper into a pad one-eighth the size of a broadsheet page.

'Five down, spicy meat jelly. ASPIC. Three across, counterfeit. BOGUS! Howzat.'

'You're in good nick,' I say. 'I would've had to rack my brains for BOGUS. Why don't you do harder ones?'

'Oh, I can't do those other ones, the cryptic.'

'You have to know Shakespeare and the Bible off by heart to do those,' I say.

'Yairs. Course, if you got hold of the answer and filled it out looking at that, with a lot of practice you could come round to their way of thinking. They used to have good ones in the *Weekly Times*. But I s'pose they had so many complaints from cockies who couldn't do 'em that they had to ease off.'

I do not feel comfortable yet about writing the postcards. It would seem graceless. I flip through my mother's pattern book.

'There's some nice ones there,' she says. 'What about the one with the floppy collar?'

'Want to buy some wool?' says my father. He tosses the finished crossword on to the coffee table and stands up with a vast yawn. 'Oh—ee—oh—ooh. Come on, Miss. I'll drive you over to Pacific Fair.'

I choose the wool and count out the number of balls specified by the pattern. My father rears back to look at it: this movement struck terror into me when I was a teenager but I now recognise it as long-sightedness.

'Pure wool, is it?' he says. As soon as he touches it he will know. He fingers it, and looks at me.

'No,' I say. 'Got a bit of synthetic in it. It's what the pattern says to use.'

'Why don't you—' He stops. Once he would have tried to prevent me from buying it. His big blunt hands used to fling out the fleeces, still warm, on to the greasy table. His hands looked as if they had no feeling in them but they teased out the wool, judged it, classed it, assigned it a fineness and a destination: Italy, Switzerland, Japan. He came home with thorns embedded deep in the flesh of his palms. He stood patiently while my mother gouged away at them with a needle. He drove away at shearing time in a yellow car with running boards, up to the big sheds in the country; we rode on the running boards as far as the corner of our street, then skipped home. He went to the Melbourne Show for work, not pleasure, and once he brought me home a plastic trumpet. 'Fordie,' he called me, and took me to the wharves and said, 'See that rope? It's not a rope. It's a hawser.' 'Hawser,' I repeated, wanting him to think I was a serious person. We walked along Strachan Avenue, Manifold Heights, hand in hand. 'Listen,' he said. 'Listen to the wind in the wires.' I must have been very little then, for the wires were so high I can't remember seeing them.

He turns away from the fluffy pink balls and waits with his hands in his pockets for me to pay.

'What do you do all day, up here?' I say on the way home.

'Oh…play bowls. Follow the real estate. I ring up the firms that advertise these flash units and I ask 'em questions. I let 'em lower and lower their price. See how low they'll go. How many more discounts they can dream up.' He drives like a farmer in a ute, leaning forward with his arms curved round the wheel, always about to squint up through the windscreen at the sky, checking the weather.

'Don't they ask your name?'

'Yep.'

'What do you call yourself?'

'Oh, Jackson or anything.' He flicks a glance at me. We begin to laugh, looking away from each other.

'It's bloody crook up here,' he says. 'Jerry-built. Sad. "Every conceivable luxury"! They can't get rid of it.

They're desperate. Come on. We'll go up and you can have a look.'

The lift in Biarritz is lined with mushroom-coloured carpet. We brace our backs against its wall and it rushes us upwards. The salesman in the display unit has a moustache, several gold bracelets, a beige suit, and a clipboard against his chest. He is engaged with an elderly couple and we are able to slip past him into the living room.

'Did you see that peanut?' hisses my father.

'A gilded youth,' I say. '"Their eyes are dull, their heads are flat, they have no brains at all."'

He looks impressed, as if he thinks I have made it up on the spot. '"The Man from Ironbark",' I add.

'I only remember "The Geebung Polo Club",' he says. He mimes leaning off a horse and swinging a heavy implement. We snort with laughter. Just inside the living room door stand five Ionic pillars in a half-moon curve. Beyond them, through the glass, are views of a river and some mountains. The river winds in a plain, the mountains are sudden, lumpy and crooked.

'From the other side you can see the sea,' says my father.

'Would you live up here?'

'Not on your life. Not with those flaming pillars.'

From the bedroom window he points out another

21

high-rise building closer to the sea. Its name is Chelsea. It is battle-ship grey with a red trim. Its windows face away from the ocean. It is tall and narrow, of mean proportions, almost prison-like. 'I wouldn't mind living in that one,' he says. I look at it in silence. He has unerringly chosen the ugliest one. It is so ugly that I can find nothing to say.

It is Saturday afternoon. My father is waiting for the Victorian football to start on TV. He rereads the paper.

'Look at this,' he says. 'Mum, remember that seminar we went to about investment in diamonds?'

'Up here?' I say. 'A *seminar*?'

'S'posed to be an investment that would double its value in six days. We went along one afternoon. They were obviously con-men. Ooh, setting up a big con, you could tell. They had sherry and sandwiches.'

'That's all we went for, actually,' says my mother.

'What sort of people went?' I ask.

'Oh…people like ourselves,' says my father.

'Do you think anybody bought any?'

'Sure. Some idiots. Anyway, look at this in today's *Age*. "The Diamond Dreamtime. World diamond market plummets." Haw haw haw.'

He turns on the TV in time for the bounce. I cast on stitches as instructed by the pattern and begin to knit. My mother and Auntie Lorna, well advanced in complicated garments for my sister's teenage children, conduct their monologues which cross, coincide and run parallel. My father mumbles advice to the footballers and emits bursts of contemptuous laughter. 'Bloody idiot,' he says.

I go to the room I am to share with Auntie Lorna and come back with the packet of postcards. When I get out my pen and the stamps and set myself up at the table my father looks up and shouts to me over the roar of the crowd, 'Given up on the knitting?'

'No. Just knocking off a few postcards. People expect a postcard when you go to Queensland.'

'Have to keep up your correspondence, Father,' says my mother.

'I'll knit later,' I say.

'How much have you done?' asks my father.

'This much.' I separate thumb and forefinger.

'Dear Philip,' I write. I make my writing as thin and small as I can: the back of the postcard, not the front, is the art form. 'Look where I am. A big red setter wet from the surf shambles up the side way of the unit, looking lost and anxious as setters always do. My parents send it packing with curses in an inarticulate tongue. Go orn, get orf, gorn!'

'Dear Philip. THE IDENTIFICATION OF THE BIRDS AND FISHES. *My father*: "Look at those albatross. They must

23

have eyes that can see for a hundred miles. As soon as one dives, they come from everywhere. Look at 'em dive! Bang! Down they go." *Me*: "What sort of fish would they be diving for?" *My father*: "Whiting. They only eat whiting." *Me*: "They do not!" *My father*: "How the hell would I know what sort of fish they are."'

'Dear Philip. My father says they are albatross, but my mother (in the bathroom, later) remarks to me that albatross have shorter, more hunched necks.'

'Dear Philip. I share a room with Auntie Lorna. She also is writing postcards and has just asked me how to spell TOO. I like her very much and *she likes me*. "I'll keep the stickybeaks in the Woomelang post office guessing," she says. "I won't put my name on the back of the envelope."'

'Dear Philip. OUTSIDE THE POST OFFICE. My father, Auntie Lorna and I wait in the car for my mother to go in and pick up the mail from the locked box. *My father*: "Gawd, amazing, isn't it, what people do. See that sign there, ENTER, with the arrow pointing upwards? What sort of a thing is that? Is it a joke, or just some no-hoper foolin' around? That woman's been in the phone box for half an hour, I bet. How'd you be, outside the public phone waiting for some silly coot to finish yackin' on about everything under the sun, while you had something important to say. That happened to us, once, up at—" My mother opens the door and gets in. "Three letters," she says. "All for me."'

Sometimes my little story overflows the available space and I have to run over on to a second postcard. This means I must find a smaller, secondary tale, or some disconnected remark, to fill up card number two.

'*Me*: (opening cupboard) "Hey! Scrabble! We can have a game of Scrabble after tea!" *My father*: (with a scornful laugh) "I can't wait."'

'Dear Philip. I know you won't write back. I don't even know whether you are still at this address.'

'Dear Philip. One Saturday morning I went to Coles and bought a scarf. It cost four and sixpence and I was happy with my purchase. He whisked it out of my hand and looked at the label. "Made in China. Is it real silk? Let's test it." He flicked on his cigarette lighter. We all screamed and my mother said, "Don't *bite*! He's only teasing you."'

'Dear Philip. Once, when I was fourteen, I gave cheek to him at the dinner table. He hit me across the head with his open hand. There was silence. My little brother gave a high, hysterical giggle and I laughed too, in shock. He hit me again. After the washing up I was sent for. He was sitting in an armchair, looking down.

"The reason why we don't get on any more," he said, "is because we're so much alike." This idea filled me with such revulsion that I turned my swollen face away. It was swollen from crying, not from the blows, whose force had been more symbolic than physical.'

'Dear Philip. Years later he read my mail. He found the contraceptive pills. He drove up to Melbourne and found me and made me come home. He told me I was letting men use my body. He told me I ought to see a psychiatrist. I was in the front seat and my mother was in the back. I thought, "If I open the door and jump out, I won't have to listen to this any more." My mother tried to stick up for me. He shouted at her. "It's your fault," he said. "You were too soft on her.'"

'Dear Philip. I know you've heard all this before. I also know it's no worse than anyone else's story.'

'Dear Philip. And again years later he asked me a personal question. He was driving, I was in the suicide seat. "What went wrong," he said, "between you and Philip?" Again I turned my face away. "I don't want to talk about it." I said. There was silence. He never asked again. And years after *that*, in a café in Paris on my way to work, far enough away from him to be able to, I thought of that question and began to cry. Dear Philip. I forgive you for everything.'

Late in the afternoon my mother and Auntie Lorna and I walk along the beach to Surfers. The tide is out: our bare feet scarcely mark the firm sand. Their two voices run on, one high, one low. If I speak they pretend to listen, just as I feign attention to their endless, looping discourses: these are our courtesies: this is love. Everything is spoken, nothing is said. On the way back I point out to them the smoky orange clouds that are massing far out to sea, low over the horizon. Obedient, they stop and face the water. We stand in a row, Auntie Lorna in a pretty frock with sandals dangling from her finger, my mother and I with our trousers rolled up. Once I asked my Brazilian friend a stupid question. He was listening to a conversation between me and a Frenchman about our countries' electoral systems. He was not speaking and, thinking to include him, I said, 'And how do people vote *chez toi,* Rubens?' He looked at me with a small smile. 'We don't have elections,' he said. Where's Rio from here? 'Look at those clouds!' I say. 'You'd think there was another city out there, wouldn't you, burning.'

Just at dark the air takes on the colour and dampness of the sub-tropics. I walk out the screen door and stand my gin on a fence post. I lean on the fence and look at the ocean. Soon the moon will thrust itself over the line. If I did a painting of a horizon, I think, I would make it look like a row of rocking, inverted Vs, because that's what I see when I look at it. The flatness of a horizon is intellectual. A cork pops on the first-floor balcony behind me. I glance up. In the half dark two men with moustaches are smiling down at me.

'Drinking champagne tonight?' I say.

'Wonderful sound, isn't it,' says the one holding the bottle.

I turn back to the moonless horizon. Last year I went camping on the Murray River. I bought the cards at Tocumwal. I had to write fast for the light was dropping and spooky noises were coming from the trees. 'Dear Dad,' I wrote. 'I am up on the Murray, sitting by the camp fire. It's nearly dark now but earlier it was beautiful, when the sun was going down and the dew was rising.' Two weeks later, at home, I received a letter from him written in his hard, rapid, slanting hand, each word ending in a sharp upward flick. The letter itself concerned a small financial matter, and consisted of two sentences on half a sheet of quarto, but on the back of the envelope he had dashed off a personal message: 'P. S. Dew does not rise. It *forms*.'

The moon does rise, as fat as an orange, out of the sea straight in front of the unit. A child upstairs sees it too and utters long werewolf howls. My mother makes a meal and we eat it. 'Going to help Mum with the dishes, are you, Miss?' says my father from his armchair. My shoulders stiffen. I am, I do. I lie on the couch and read an old *Woman's Day*. Princess Caroline of Monaco wears a black dress and a wide white hat. The knitting needles make their mild clicking. Auntie Lorna and my father come from the same town, Hopetoun in the Mallee, and when the news is over they begin again.

'I always remember the cars of people,' says my father. 'There was an old four-cylinder Dodge, belonging to Whatsisname. It had—'

'Would that have been one of the O'Lachlans?' says Auntie Lorna.

'Jim O'Lachlan. It had a great big exhaust pipe coming out the back. And I remember stuffing a potato up it.'

'A *potato*?' I say.

'The bloke was a councillor,' says my father. 'He came out of the Council chambers and got into the Dodge and started her up. He only got fifty yards up the street when BA—BANG! This damn thing shot out the back—I reckon it's still going!' He closes his lips and drops his head back against the couch to hold in his laughter.

I walk past Biarritz, where globes of light float among shrubbery, and the odd balcony on the half-empty tower holds rich people out into the creamy air. A barefoot man

29

steps out of the take-away food shop with a hamburger in his hand. He leans against the wall to unwrap it, and sees me hesitating at the slot of the letterbox, holding up the postcards and reading them over and over in the weak light from the public phone. 'Too late to change it now,' he calls. I look up. He grins and nods and takes his first bite of the hamburger. Beside the letterbox stands a deep rubbish bin with a swing lid. I punch open the bin and drop the postcards in.

All night I sleep safely in my bed. The waves roar and hiss, and slam like doors. Auntie Lorna snores, but when I tug at the corner of her blanket she sighs and turns over and breathes more quietly. In the morning the rising sun hits the front windows and floods the place with a light so intense that the white curtains can hardly net it. Everything is pink and golden. In the sink a cockroach lurks. I try to swill it down the drain with a cup of water but it resists strongly. The air is bright, is milky with spray. My father is already up: while the kettle boils he stands out on the edge of the grass, the edge of his property, looking at the sea.

THE DARK, THE LIGHT

WE HEARD HE was back. We heard he was staying in a swanky hotel. We heard she was American. We washed our hair. We wore what we thought was appropriate. We waited for him to declare himself. We waited for him to call.

No calls came. We discussed his probable whereabouts, the meaning of his silence, the possibilities of his future.

We thought we saw him getting into a taxi outside the Rialto, outside the Windsor, outside the Regent, outside the Wentworth, outside the Stock Exchange, outside the Diorama. Was it him? What was he wearing? What did he have on? A tweed jacket, black shoes. Even in summer? His idea of this town is cold. He's been away. He's lost the feel of it. He's been in Europe. He's been in America. He's been in the tropics. He's left. He's gone. He doesn't live here any more. He's only visiting. He's only passing through. Was his face white? His shirt was white. His hair was longer. Did you see her? She wasn't there. He was on his own.

We saw them in a club. We saw her. She was blond. They were both blond. They were together. They were dressed in white, in cream, in gold, in thousands of dollars' worth of linen and leather. They sat at a table with their backs to the wall. The wall was dark. They were light. Their hair and their garments shone. They knew things we did not know, they owned things we had never heard of. They were from somewhere else. They were not from here. They were from further north, from the sunny place, the blue and yellow place, the sparkling place, the water place. They were from the capital. More than one of us had to be led away weeping. He's gone. He won't live here again. He has left us behind. He has gone away and left us in the cold. The music stopped and they got up and left and the door closed. We stood in our dark club in our dark clothes.

Invitations came, but not many. Hardly any. Very few. Did you get one? Neither did I. Maybe the mail… a strike…a bottleneck at the exchange…There were very few. Only three or four. Will you go? Of course not. It wouldn't be right. It would hurt, it would be wrong, I couldn't do it, I wouldn't be able to live with myself, I would lose friends, I wouldn't be seen dead, if you don't I won't either, it's a moral issue, I couldn't possibly.

What happened up there? Did you go? Did you hear? What was it like? Tell us what happened. It was summer, he was early, she was late, she made an entrance, the bells were ringing, the organ thundered, his hair lay in stiff sculpted curls, she was all in cream, her hair was up, she was choked with pearls, his family was there, the church was packed, he gave her his arm, they stood sides touching. The minister threw back his head and shouted *Come into their hearts Lord Jesus!* The guests were embarrassed, they fluffed their bobs, they brushed their shoulders, they read the brass plaques, it was religious, it was low church, it was not what we thought, we imagined something else, it was not his style, it was a bit much, it was over the top, it was a church after all and what did you expect, the guests were clever, they knew better, they were modern, they sat in the pews and sneered.

And afterwards? Outside? The trees were covered in leaves and threaded with coloured lights, it was night in the garden, the air was warm, the night was tender, French at least we thought, we thought French, we held out our glasses, the waiters twirled among us, the bottles were napkinned, it was local, we had hoped for better, we drank it anyway, we became more grateful, the families stood in line, they shook our hands, they welcomed us, we were ashamed of our ingratitude. We saw him standing alone for a moment under a tree, we stepped quickly towards him to show him we had come, we had come a very long way, we had come to show him we had come, to deliver the compliments, to bring the greetings of the other place, we stepped up, we reached out, our fingers touched his elbow and she came swooping all creamy with pearls, he spun on one heel, his hands opened, he showed us his palms, he smiled, he melted, he was no longer there, he was gone, the trees were covered in leaves, their branches were threaded with coloured lights, our clothes were stiff, our clothes were dark, our clothes came from the other place, and we too came from the other place, we put down our glasses, we turned away, we turned to go back to the other place, we turned and went back to the other place, we went without bitterness, humbly we went away.

IN PARIS

THE APARTMENT WAS on the fourth floor. The building had no lift. On his day off the man lay on the mattress that served as a sofa and read, slowly and carefully, all the newspapers of his city. The tall windows were open on to the balcony. Every twenty minutes a bus swerved in to the stop down below, and the curtain puffed past his face. At two o'clock the woman came into the living room with her boots on.

'I feel like going for a walk,' she said.

'Bon. D'accord,' said the man.

'Want to come with me?'

'Tu vas où?'

'Up to Sacré Coeur and back. Not far.'

'Ouf,' said the man. 'All those steps.' He put one paper down and unfolded the next.

'Oh, come on,' said the woman. 'Won't you come? I'm bored.'

'I don't want to go down into the street,' said the man. 'I have to go down there every day. I get sick of it. Today I feel like staying home.'

The woman pulled a dead leaf off the pot plant. 'Just for an hour?' she said.

'Too many tourists,' said the man. 'You go. I'll have a little sleep. Anyway it's going to rain.'

Late in the afternoon the man went into the kitchen and opened the refrigerator. He looked inside it, then shut it again. He walked across the squeaking parquet to the bedroom. The woman was lying on her stomach reading a book by the light of a shaded lamp. Her wet boots stood in the corner by the window.

'There's nothing to eat,' said the man. 'No one went to the market.'

The woman looked up. 'What about the fish?'

'Yes, the fish is there.'

'We can eat the fish, then.'

'There's nothing to have with it.'

The woman marked her place with one finger.

'What happened to the brussels sprouts?' she said. 'Did the others eat them last night?'

'No.'

'Well, let's have fish and brussels sprouts.'

Before she had finished the sentence the man was shaking his head.

'Why not?'

'Fish and green vegetables are never eaten together.'

'What?'

'They are not eaten together.'

The woman closed the book. 'People have salad with fish. That's green.'

'Salad is different. Salad is a separate course. It is not served on the same plate.'

'Can you explain to me,' said the woman, 'the reason why fish and green vegetables must not be eaten together?'

The man looked at his hand against the white wall. 'It is not done,' he said. 'They do not complement each other. Fish and potatoes, yes. Frites. Pommes de terre au four. But not green vegetables.'

'It's getting on for dinner time,' said the woman. She turned on her back and clasped her hands behind her head. 'The others will be back soon.'

'I don't know what to do,' said the man. He moved his feet closer together and pushed his hands into his pockets.

'If I were you,' said the woman. 'If I were you and it was my turn to cook, and if there was nothing to eat except fish and green vegetables, do you know what I'd do? I'd cook fish and green vegetables. That's what I'd do.'

'Ecoute,' said the man. 'There are always good chemical and aesthetic reasons behind customs.'

'Yes, but what *are* they.'

'I'm sure if we looked it up in the *Larousse Gastro-nomique* it would be explained.'

The woman got off the low bed and went to the window in her socks and T-shirt. She looked out.

'I'm hungry,' she said. 'Where I come from, we just eat what's there.'

'And it is not a secret,' said the man, 'that where you come from the food is barbaric.'

The woman kept her back to the room. 'My mother cooked nice food. We had nice meals.'

'Chops,' said the man. 'Hamburgers. I heard you telling my mother. "La bouffe est dégueulasse," you said. That's what you said.'

'I said "était". It was. It used to be. But it's not any more. It's not now.'

The man took a set of keys out of his pocket and began to flip them in and out of his palm.

'Aren't there any onions?' said the woman, still looking out the window.

'No. Not even onions.'

'I don't see,' said the woman, 'that you've got any choice. What choice have you got? Unless you cook the fish by itself, or just the sprouts.'

'There would not be enough for everybody.'

The woman turned round from the grey window. 'Why don't you go out into the kitchen and cook it up. Cook what's there. Just cook it up and see what happens. And if the others don't like it they can take their custom elsewhere.'

The man took a deep breath. He put the keys back in his pocket. He scratched his head until his hair stood up in a crest. 'J'ai mal fait mon marché,' he said. 'I should have planned better. We should have—'

'For God's sake,' said the woman. She leaned against the closed window. 'What's the matter with you? It's only food.'

The man put his bare foot on the edge of the mattress and bounced it once, twice.

'Tu vois?' he said. 'Tu vois comment tu es? "Only food." No French person would ever, ever say "It's only food".'

'But it *is* only food,' said the woman. 'In the final analysis that's what it *is*. It's to keep us alive. It's to stop us from feeling hungry for a couple of hours so we can get our minds off our stomachs and go about our business. And all the rest is only decoration.'

'Oh là là,' said the man. 'Tu es—'

He flattened his hair with one hand, and let his hand fall to his side. Then he turned and walked back into the kitchen. He opened the refrigerator. The fish lay on its side on a white plate. He opened the cupboard under the window. The brussels sprouts, cupped in their shed outer leaves, sat on a paper bag on the bottom shelf. The man stood in the middle of the room and looked from one open door to the other, and back again.

LITTLE HELEN'S
SUNDAY AFTERNOON

LATE ON A winter Sunday afternoon, Little Helen stood behind her mother on the verandah of Noah's house. Her mother raised her finger to the buzzer but the door opened from the inside and Noah's father came hurrying out.

'Bad luck, girls,' he said. He was pulling on his jacket. 'Just got a call from Northern General. Some kid's cut his finger off.'

'His whole finger?' said Little Helen. 'Right off?'

'I hope someone slung it in the icebox,' said Little Helen's mother. 'What a time to make you work.'

'*Unpaid* work,' said Noah's mother. 'Will I save you some soup, Jim?'

'Let's see,' said Noah's father. 'Four thirty. I'll have to do a graft. Five thirty, six, six thirty. Yeah. Save me some.'

As he talked he walked, and was already in the car. The drive was full of coloured leaves.

Little Helen's mother and Noah's were sisters and liked to shriek a lot when visiting.

'Little Helen!' said Noah's mother. 'Jump up! Let me have a hold of you!'

Little Helen stepped out from behind her mother, bent her knees, raised her arms and sprang. Noah's mother caught her, but staggered and gave a cry. 'Ark! You used to be such a fairy little thing. Last time you were here you sat on my knee and do you know what you said? You said, "I *love* being small!"'

Little Helen went red and dropped her eyes. She saw her own foot, in its large, strapped blue shoe, swinging awkwardly near her aunt's hip.

'Come on, Meg,' said Little Helen's mother. 'Let's pop into the bedroom. I've got some business to conduct. It's in this bag.'

Noah's mother unclasped her hands under Little Helen's bottom and let her slide to the ground.

'Another hair shirt, is it,' she said to Little Helen's mother. 'I suppose I'll be left holding the baby.'

'What are you going to call it if it's a boy?' said Little Helen.

The women looked at each other. Their cheeks puffed out and their lips went tight. They went into the bedroom and closed the door without answering her question. Little Helen could hear them screeching and crashing round in front of the mirror. She knew that it was not a hair shirt at all, but a pair of shoes her mother had paid a lot of money for and worn once then discovered they were too big, and which she hoped that Noah's mother would buy from her. Little Helen brushed the back of her tartan skirt down flat and stood in the hallway. She saw her own feet parallel. She thought of a waitress. It was a long time ago, in the dining room of the Bull and Mouth Hotel in Stawell. The waitress was quite old and she stood patiently, holding her order pad and pencil, while Little Helen's father took a long time to make up his mind what to have. Little Helen, who always had roast lamb, tried to stop looking at the waitress's feet, but could not. There was nothing special about the feet. But the neatness of their position, two inches apart and perfectly parallel on the carpet's green and orange flowers, caused

Little Helen to experience a painful sadness. She decided to have chicken instead.

'Chicken's pretty risky,' said her father.

'I want chicken, though,' said Little Helen.

She got chicken. It was all right but rather dry. She ate more of it than she wanted.

'How's the chicken?' said her father.

'A bit risky,' said Little Helen.

Her father laughed so much that everyone at the other tables turned to stare.

Little Helen knew she was clever but she noticed that words did not always bear the same simple, serious meaning that they had at school when she copied them into her exercise book. On her spelling list she had the word 'capacious' to put into a sentence. 'The elephant is a capacious beast,' she wrote. Her mother's mouth trembled when Little Helen showed her the twenty finished sentences, in best writing and ruled off. She explained why 'capacious' was not quite right. Her polite kindness and her trembling mouth made Little Helen blush until tears filled her eyes.

Little Helen stood outside her aunt's bedroom and waited for something to happen. Time became elastic, and sagged. She hated visiting. She had to be dragged away from her wooden table, her full set of Derwents, her different inks and textas, her special paper-cutting scissors, her rulers and sharpeners and rubbers. The teacher never gave her enough homework. She could have worked all weekend.

She did not like the feeling of other people's houses. There was nothing to do. Pieces of furniture stood sparsely in chilly rooms. The long stretches of skirting board were empty of meaning, and the kitchen smells were mournful, as if the saucepans on the stove contained nothing but grey bones boiling for a soup.

The bedroom door opened and Little Helen's mother poked her head out. She had been laughing. Her face was pink and she was wearing nothing but a bra and pants and a black hat like a box with a bit of net hanging over her eyes.

'We're having dress-ups,' she said. 'Want to come in and play?'

Little Helen was embarrassed and shook her head. They didn't know how to play properly. They were much too tall and had real bosoms, and they talked all the time about how much they had paid for the clothes and where they would go to wear them, instead of being serious and thoughtful about what the clothes meant in the game.

'Oh, don't be so unsociable!' said her mother. 'Go and see Noah.'

'He won't want to see me,' said Little Helen. 'Anyway I don't know where he is.'

'He's out the back,' shouted his mother from inside the bedroom. 'Probably making something. Some white elephant or other.'

They started to laugh again, and Little Helen's mother went back into the bedroom and slammed the door.

Little Helen plodded down the hall and entered the kitchen. The lunch dishes were all over the sink. Between the stacked plates she found quite a lot of tinned sweet corn, crusted with cold butter. She put her mouth down to the china and sucked up the scrapings. Her palate took on a coating of grease. She moved over to the pantry cupboard and helped herself to five Marie biscuits, some peeled almonds, four squares of cooking chocolate and a handful of crystallised ginger. Eating fast and furtively, bolting the food inside the big dark cupboard, she started to get that rude and secret feeling of wanting to do a shit. She crossed her legs and squeezed her bum shut, and went on guzzling. A little salvo of farts escaped into her pants and if something funny had occurred to her at that moment she would not have been able to hang on; but she kept her mind on that poor boy who had cut his finger off, and gradually she felt the lump go back up inside her for later.

If she ate any more she would spoil her tea. She hitched up her skirt, wiped her palms on her pants, and set out across the kitchen towards the wide glass door.

Noah's yard was long and sloped steeply down to the back fence. The trees had no leaves, and from the porch steps Little Helen could see for miles and miles, as far as the centre of the city. She paused to stare at the tiny bunch of skyscrapers, like a city in a film, and at the long curved bridge beyond them with its chain of lights already flicking on. The afternoon was nearly over. It was not raining now. Water lay in puddles on the sky-blue plastic cover of the swimming pool. The branches of bare bushes were a glossy black, like a licked pencil lead.

Little Helen's feet sank into the spongy grass. Her shoes looked very large and blue on the greenness. The grass was so green that it made her feel sick. The sky was low. An unnatural light leaked out of the clouds, and the chords the light played were in the same dull, complicated key as the grass-sickness. The air did not move. It was cold. Her legs felt white and thin under the pleated skirt.

Grass grew right up to the shed door, which was shut. Noah must be in there. She stood outside it and paid attention. There was a noise like somebody using sandpaper on a piece of wood, but softer; like two people using sandpaper, two rhythms not quite hitting the same beat. Someone laughed.

Little Helen saw a red plastic bucket half under the shed. She pulled it out and turned it upside down. Its bottom was cracked and it was almost too weak to hold her, but by keeping her shoes on the very outside of its rim she could balance on it and get her head up to the window. Rags had been hooked across it on the inside, and only one small corner was uncovered. She put her eye to it. It was even darker inside. In there the night had already begun. How could he see what he was doing?

She shifted her left foot on the bucket and missed the rim. The toe of her shoe pierced the split base. Her fingers lost their hold on the windowsill. A fierce sharpness scraped through her sock and raked its claws up her shin. She swivelled sideways with a grunt, lurched against the shed wall, and stumbled out on to the lawn. Shocked and gasping, she found herself still upright, but with the red bucket clamped round her left leg just below the knee.

In the upper part of the sky, above the bunch of skyscrapers, the clouds split like rotten cloth and let a flat blade of light through. It leaned between sky and earth, a crooked pillar. Little Helen took a breath. She clenched her fists. She opened her mouth and bellowed.

'Noah!'

There was a silence, then a harsh scrabbling inside the shed.

'Come out!' bawled Little Helen. 'Come out and see me! It's not fair! I'm tired of waiting!'

Her shin was stinging very hard, as if her mother had already pressed on to the broken skin the Listerine-soaked cotton wool. Her invisible left sock felt wet. Little Helen thought, 'I could easily be crying.' The shed door was wrenched open and a huge boy with red hair and skin like boiled custard burst through. He was croaking.

'You were spying! Who said you could spy on me?'

Something strange had happened to Noah, and not only to his voice. The whole shape of his head had changed. He didn't look like a boy any more. He looked like a dog, or a fish. His eyes were like slits, and had moved higher up his face and outwards into his temples.

'Look, Noah,' whispered Little Helen. She was not sure whether she meant the drunken pillar of light or the bucket on her leg. He took three steps towards her and grabbed her by the arm. She jerked her face away from the smell of him: not just sweaty but raw, like steak.

'If you tell what you saw,' he choked. Red patches flared low on his speckled cheeks.

'It was dark,' said Little Helen. She could feel blood

running down into her cotton sock. 'I couldn't even see in. I couldn't see anything. I only heard the noise. I promise.'

He dragged her towards the shed door. The grass squelched under his thick-soled jogging shoes. She had to stagger with her legs apart because of the bucket, but he did not notice it, and pushed her up the step. Another boy was standing just inside. Their great bodies, panting and stinking, filled the shed.

'Don't bring her in here, you fuckwit!' said the other boy. His shoelaces were undone and he was doing up his trousers. 'I'm going home.'

The shed smelt of cigarettes. They must have smoked a whole packet. They would get lung cancer. They would get into really bad trouble. The other boy bent to tie his lace and Little Helen saw that there was a third person in the shed. A girl was sitting on a sleeping bag that was spread out on the floor. She was pulling on her boots. As she scrambled to her feet she spotted Little Helen's bucket. She stopped on all fours in dog position and looked up into Little Helen's face. Her eyes were caked with black stuff and her hair was stiff, like burnt grass. She laughed; Little Helen could see all her back teeth.

'Ha!' said the girl. 'Now you know what happens to people who snoop. Come on, Justin. Let's go.'

She stood up and buckled her belt. The two of them barged out the door. Little Helen heard their feet thumping on the grass and then crunching on the gravel drive.

'I know what *you've* been doing,' said Little Helen. The butts were everywhere. Some had lipstick on the yellow end.

'Shut your face,' said Noah. In the grey light from the open door his head with its short orange hair and flat temples was as smooth and savage as a bull terrier's. He gave a high snigger. 'You look stupid with that bucket on your leg.'

The moment for crying was long gone. She would have had to fake it, though she knew she had the right. 'It hurts,' said Little Helen. 'I can feel blood still coming out. It hurts quite a lot, actually. It might be serious.'

'You want to know about blood?' said Noah. His small, high, dog's eyes began to glow, as if a weak torch battery had flicked on inside his head. 'I'll show you what can happen to people.'

'I think I'd better speak to my mother,' said Little Helen. 'I need to ask her about something very important.'

'First I'll show you something,' said Noah.

'I can't walk,' said Little Helen. She folded her arms and stood square, with her knees apart to accommodate the bucket, but he scooped her off the ground in one round movement and ran out of the shed and across the garden.

From her sideways and horizontal position Little Helen saw the grassy world bounce and swing. She kept her left leg stuck out straight so the bucket would not be interfered with. His big hip and thigh worked under her waist like a horse's. He took the back steps in a couple of bounds. At the top he swung her across his front while he fumbled with the glass door, and in its broad pane she saw reflected her own white underpants, twisted half off her bottom, and down in its lower corner, half-obscured by the image of her faithful bucket, the bunch of skyscrapers flaming with light. She writhed to cover her pants and his hard fingers gripped her tighter. He forged through the kitchen, along the passage and into a small dim room that smelt of leather and Finepoint pens with their caps off.

Dumped, she staggered for the door, but he got past her and kicked it shut.

'Mum!' said Little Helen, without conviction.

'Look,' said Noah. He kept one foot against the door and reached behind her to a large, low, wooden cupboard that stood on legs against one wall. He slid open its front panel and switched on a light inside it.

It was not a cupboard. It was a box. It was deep, and it

was full of pictures, tiny square ones, suspended in space, arranged in neat horizontal rows and lit gently from behind so that they glowed in many colours, jewel-like, but mostly yellow, brown and red. The magical idea, the bright orderliness of it, took Little Helen's breath away. She limped forward, smiling, favouring her bucketed leg. Noah left the door and crouched beside her. He must have forgiven her: he was panting from his run, from his haste to bring her to this wonder.

The pictures were slides. They seemed to be of children's faces. But there was something unusual about them. Were they children in face paint? Were they dressed in Costumes of Other Lands, or at a Hat Competition? Were they disguised as angels, or fairies? Little Helen tried to kneel, but her bucket bothered her. She spread her legs wide and bent them, and opened her arms to keep her balance. In this Balinese posture she lowered herself to contemplate the mystery.

The children were horrible. Their heads were bloodied. Their hair had been torn out by the roots, their scalps were raw and crisscrossed with black railway lines. Their lips were blue and swollen and bulged outwards, barely contained by stitches. Their eyes had burst like pickled onions, their foreheads were stove in, their chins were crushed to pink pulp. One baby, too new to sit up, had a huge purple furry thing growing from its temple to its chin. Another had two dark holes instead of a nose and its top lip was not there at all.

But the worst thing was that not a single one of them was crying. The ones whose eyes still worked looked straight at Little Helen with a patient, sober gaze. They were not surprised that these terrible things had happened to them, that their mothers had turned away at the wrong moment, that the war had come, that men with guns and knives had got into the house and found them. Little Helen's hackles went lumpy and her stomach rose into her throat. She shut her eyes and tried to straighten up, but Noah put his hand down hard on her shoulder and croaked, 'See that kid there? A power line fell on him. His brain woulda blown right out of his skull.'

Little Helen squirmed out from under his hand and crawled away. He did not follow her, but watched her drag her bucket to the door and stand up and reach the high handle. She got her good foot out into the hall and looked back. He was crouching before the picture box. The soft white light from inside it polished his furry hair. Little Helen saw that he could not stop looking at the pictures. He turned to her.

'See?' he said. 'See what can happen to little kids?'

She nodded.

'Don't you like it?' The dim torch battery went on behind his eyes. He was smiling. 'You don't, do you. Piss weak. Look at this equipment. Best that money can buy.'

'What—' She cleared her throat. 'Did they all die?'

'Die? Course they didn't die. My dad sewed 'em up. But they were very sick. And afterwards they were always ugly. For the rest of their lives.'

Little Helen let go the door handle and slid out into the hallway. Her palms were sticky and the backs of her hands had shrunk and gone hard, but she was not going to be sick. She stumped away down the passage towards the front of the house. The bucket made a soft clunk with every second step.

Her mother and Noah's were sitting quietly on the edge of the big double bed. They were dressed in their ordinary clothes and sat with their hands folded in their laps as if waiting for something. Little Helen clumped into the doorway and stopped. They looked up. She saw their two white faces, round and flat as dinner plates, shining above their dark dresses in what remained of the light.

LA CHANCE EXISTE

I AM THE kind of person who always gets stopped at Customs. Julie says it's because I can't keep my eyes still. 'You look as if you're constantly checking the whereabouts of the exits,' she said. She'll never really trust me again, I suppose. It shits me but I can't blame her. I love her, that's all, and I feel like serving her.

When we got to Boulogne we had to hang around for three hours waiting for the ferry because of a strike on the other side. I would have sat in a café and read *Le Monde*, but Julie wanted to walk round and look at things, seeing she'd only been in France a couple of days.

Her French was hopeless and she was too proud to try. When I met her plane at Orly she was already agitated about not being able to understand. We went straight to a bar in the airport and she insisted on ordering. The waiter, tricked by her good accent, made a friendly remark which seemed to require an answer: her face went rigid with panic and she turned away. The waiter shrugged and went back behind the counter. She hit the table with her fist and groaned between clenched teeth. 'It's pathetic! I should be able to! I'm not stupid!'

'For Christ's sake, woman,' I said. 'You've only been in the country fifteen minutes. What do you *want* from yourself?'

Boulogne was dismal, as I had predicted. I kept telling her we should go south, down to Italy where she'd never been, but she had to go to London, she said, to meet this bloke she'd fallen in love with just before she left Australia. He was coming after her, she was dying to see him again. She fell in love with this guy, who was a musician, because at a gig she found him between sets sitting by himself in a sort of booth thing reading a book called *The Meaning of Meaning*. She told me he was extremely thin. It sounded like a disaster to me. Love will not survive a channel crossing, I pointed out, let alone the thirty-six hours from Melbourne to

London. But I was so glad to be with her again, and she wasn't listening.

We walked, in our Paris boulevard shoes, over the lumpy cobbles of Boulogne. We found a huge archway which led on to a beaten dirt track that curved round the outside of the old city, at the foot of its high walls. Julie was excited. 'It's old! It must have been trying to be impregnable!' The track was narrow. 'Single file, Indian style,' she chanted, charging ahead of me.

It was eleven o'clock on a weekday morning in July, and there was no one about. A nippy breeze came up off the channel. The water was grey and disturbed, a sea of shivers.

We tramped along merrily for twenty minutes, round the shoulder of the hill the old city stood on, turning back now and then to look at the view. The track became narrower.

'Let's go back,' I said. 'You can't see the sea round this side. It stinks.'

'Not yet. Look. What are those caravans down there?'

'I dunno. Gipsies or something. Come on, Julie.'

She pressed on. The track was hardly a track at all: it was brambly, and was obviously about to run out against a wing of a castle about a hundred yards ahead. I was ten steps behind her when she gave a sharp cry of disgust and stopped dead. I caught up with her. There was a terrible smell, of shit and things rotting. At her feet was the mangled corpse of a large bird: it looked as if it had been torn to bits. Its head was a yard away from its neck, half its beak had been wrenched off, and there were dirty feathers everywhere, stuck in the spiky bushes, fluttering in the seawind. The shit was human. Its shapes were man-made; it was meat-eater's shit, foul.

We looked at each other. The murder was fresh. In the crisp breeze the feathers on the creature's breast riffled and subsided like an expensive haircut. It was very quiet up there.

'Someone's looking at us from one of those caravans,' said Julie without moving her lips. 'This is their shitting place. It's their fucking dunny. They must be laughing at us.' She gave a high-pitched giggle, pushed past me, and ploughed away through the prickly bushes, back the way we'd come.

Back amongst houses, we stood at the top of an alley in the depths of which two little boys were engaged in a complicated, urgent game with a ball and a piece of rope. One dropped his end in annoyance and walked away. The other, who had glasses and a fringe and a white face, sang out after him, in a voice clear enough for even Julie to understand.

'*La chance exis—te!*'

'What a sophisticated remark,' said Julie.

On the boat, when it finally turned up, we didn't even have the money for a drink. The sky and the sea were grey. The line between them tilted this way and that.

'Will it be rough?' said Julie. 'What if I spew?'

'You won't spew. We'll walk around and talk to each other. I'll keep your mind off your stomach.'

My glasses are the kind that are supposed to adapt automatically to the intensity of the light, but they failed to go clear again when we went down into the inside part of the ship. Cheap rubbish. The downstairs part was badly lit. I hate going back to England. I hate being able to understand everything that's going on around me. I miss that feeling of your senses having to strain an inch beyond your skin that you get in places where people aren't speaking your language.

Julie darted down the stairs and grabbed a couple of seats. We got out books and kicked our bags under the little table. On the wall near us was the multilingual sign warning passengers about the danger of rabies and the fines you get. Julie knelt up on her seat and read it with interest.

'Rabies. What's that in French. *La rage.* Ha. You don't have to be a dog to die of *that.*'

Julie is suspicious, and full of disgust. When she laughs you see that one of her back teeth is missing on the left side. If she chooses you she loves you fiercely, lashes you if you fail yourself. A faint air of contempt hangs about her even when she's in good spirits. She says she's never going home. Everyone always says that when they first get here.

She flung herself round into the seat. 'I saw Lou just before I left Melbourne,' she said. 'I told him I'd be seeing you. He laughed. He said, "*That* fuckin' little poofter!"' She glanced sideways.

'News travels fast.' I knew that's what Lou would have said. It made me tired. He could do the dope and the bum cheques on his own now. I took a breath and went in at the deep end.

'When I first got here,' I said, 'I knew I was going to have to do something. That's what I came for. I used to walk around Paris all night, looking for men and running away from them. For example. One night I was in the metro. It was packed and I was standing up holding on to one of those vertical chrome poles. A boy got on at Clignancourt. He squeezed through the crowd to the pole.

'He wasn't looking at me, but I could feel him— I might've been imagining it, but warmth passed between us. I was burning all down one side. My heart was

70

thumping. His hand on the pole was so close to my mouth I could have kissed it. The train was swaying, all the people were swaying, and I edged my hand up the pole till it was almost touching his. I felt sick, I wanted to touch him so much. I could smell his skin. I thought I was going to pass out. Then at the next stop he calmly let go of the pole and pushed through the crowd and got off.'

Julie put her feet up on the low table between us and folded her arms round her legs and laid her head sideways on her knees. She was having trouble controlling her mouth. 'What's your favourite name of a metro station?' she said.

'What? I don't know. Trocadéro.'

'Mine's Château d'Eau.'

'Ever been up on top of that station? You'd hate it. It's not safe for women.'

'Remember that time you shat on my green Lois Lane jacket?'

'It was an accident! I had diarrhoea!'

'You were so busy looking at yourself in the mirror you didn't know you were standing on my clothes.'

'The dry cleaner got it off! Why do you have to remind me?'

'"It's dog mess," you said to the lady at the dry cleaner. Dog *mess*.' She gave a snort of laughter.

'It came off, anyway.' I opened the newspaper and rattled it.

'Being homosexual must mean something,' she said. 'What happens? Is everything possible?'

'How do you mean?' Was she going to ask me what we did? I'd tell her. I'd tell her anything.

'I mean, if both of you have the same equipment does that mean it's more equal? Do people fall into habits of fucking or being fucked? Or does everyone do everything?'

'It's not really all that different,' I said, feeling shy but trying to be helpful. 'Not when you're in a relationship, anyway.'

'Oh.' She looked disappointed, and stared out the porthole at the grey sky and the grey water. Her cardigan sleeves were pushed up to her elbows and I could see the mist of blond hairs that fogged her skin. Her legs were downy like that, too. We can wear each other's clothes. She's the same height as me, with slightly more cowboy-like hips: light passes between the tops of her thighs.

'I never want to fuck with anyone unless it puts me in danger,' she said suddenly. 'I don't mean physical. I mean unless there's a chance they'll make me sad.'

'Break your heart.'

'I'll never get married. Or even live with anyone again, probably.'

'What about shithead? The bass player? Isn't that why we're making this fucking trip?'

'Are you afraid of getting old?' she said in a peculiar voice.

'My hair's starting to recede.' I pulled it back off my forehead to show her.

'Oh, bullshit. What are you, twenty-five? Look at your little round forehead. A pretty little globe.'

'And I'm getting hairs on my back,' I said, 'like my father.' I didn't mention that I twist round in front of the bathroom mirror with the tweezers in my hand.

'Can't we afford one drink and share it?' she said.

'No. We have to get the bus to Rowena's.'

'Last week,' she said, her head still on her knees, 'I was in the Louvre. I was upstairs, heading along one of the main galleries. I saw this young bloke sitting on a bench with a little pack on his back. He was about your age, English I'd say. He looked tired, and lonely, and he gave me a look. I wanted to go and sit next to him and say, "Will we go and have a cup of coffee? Or talk to each other?" But I was too…I kept walking and went down the steps to the room where all those Rubens paintings are, of Louis Whichever-it-was and Marie de Medici.

I stayed in there for ten minutes walking round, and I hated the paintings, they made me feel like spewing—all those pursed-up little mouths smirking. I went back up the steps and the boy was gone.'

The boat heaved on towards Folkestone.

'Why is it so hard to talk about sex?' she said, almost in tears. 'Every time you think you're close to saying what you mean, your mind just veers away from it, and you say something that's not quite the point.'

What would they know here about summer? The wind was sharp. People in the queue had blue lips. I was stopped before we got anywhere near Customs, this time by a smart bastard in plain clothes who was cruising up and down the bedraggled line of tourists with passports in their hands.

'His *jacket*,' muttered Julie. It was orange and black hounds-tooth. 'My God. What's happened to this country?'

'Don't get me started on that subject.' I stood still and proffered my bag. Some look must appear on my face in their presence, or maybe it's the smell of fear they say dogs can pick up. He was nasty in that bored way; idle malice. No point getting hot under the collar. While he rooted through our bags, and Julie stood with her arms folded and her chin up and her eyes far away over his garish shoulder, he asked her an impertinent question.

'How long've you known this feller?'

'I beg your pardon?'

'I said, how long've you known this feller you're travelling with?'

You can't take that tone to a woman these days. 'What's that got to do with you?' said Julie.

He stopped rummaging and looked up at her, with one of her shirts in his hand. God, she still had that old pink thing with the mended collar. He narrowed his eyes and let his slot of a mouth drop open half an inch. Here's a go, he was thinking. I kicked her ankle. She reached out, took the pink shirt and said, folding it as skilfully as a salesgirl in Georges, 'Six years or so. Nice jacket. Is that Harris?'

He wasn't quite stupid enough to answer. He shoved the pink shirt back in among the other garments and walked away. Our bags stood unzipped, sprouting private objects.

On the train to London I read and she stared at people. At Leicester Square we ran down the stairs into the tube. I caught the eye of a good-looking boy who was coming up. I turned to look back at him as he passed and she slashed me across the face with her raincoat. The zip got me near the eye.

'What did you—' I yelled.

She was laughing furiously. 'You should have seen the look on your face.'

'What look?'

'Like *this*.' She pulled a face: mouth half-open, eyes rolling up and to one side, like a dim-witted whore.

In the basement room we were supposed to keep the wooden shutters closed because Rowena said there was a prowler who stood up on the windowsill. But the room was dim and stuffy. I took off my clothes, then slid the window up and shoved open the top half of the slatted shutter. Julie whipped off her dress and stared at me.

'You still look like a little goat,' she said. 'Pan, up on his hind legs.'

I got under the sheet. 'Come on. Let's go to sleep.'

'I'm all speeded up. I'm looking for something to read.'

'Well, don't rustle the pages all night.' I turned on my side and closed my eyes. When she got into the bed she hardly weighed it down at all.

'Talk to me,' she said behind me.

I flipped over on to my back and saw she was lying there with her hands under her head. 'What'll I say?'

'Do you get just as miserable as you used to when you were straight?'

'Are you kidding?'

She shifted so that the sides of our legs touched lightly, all the way down. 'Come on. Talk.'

'Maybe more miserable,' I said. 'It's all real now. Before, I was in a dream for years, even when I was with you. Everything was blurred and messy. Now I know exactly what I want, and I also know I'll never get it.'

'Oh hell.'

'What?'

'What *do* you want?'

'Everything. I want to love some man forever and at the same time I want to fuck everyone I see. Some days I could fuck trees. Lamp posts! Dogs! The air!'

She whistled a little tune, and laughed.

'In the Tuileries,' I said, 'there is a powdery white dust.'

'What else?'

'It's a cruising place at night. Not that part with the rows of trees: they lock that. The part between the gates and the Maillol statues. I love it.'

'Why?'

'It's like a dance. It's mysterious. People move together and apart, no one speaks, everyone's faceless. It's terrifically exciting, and graceful. The point of it is nothing to do with *who*.'

Her face was quite calm, her eyes raised to the ceiling. Turning my head I could see pale freckles, a gold sleeper, a series of tiny parallel cracks in her lower lip. The skin of her leg felt very much alive to me, almost humming with life.

'Once,' she said, 'I was coming down that narrow winding staircase in one of the towers of Notre Dame. Two American blokes were coming down behind me, and I heard one of them say, "Hey! This is *steep*! My depth perception is shot already!"'

We rolled towards each other and into each other's arms. I pushed myself against her belly, pushed my face into her neck and she took me in her arms, in her legs. I cooled myself on her. Her limbs were as strong as mine. Her face hung over me and blurred in the dim room. I could smell her open flesh, she smelled like metal, salty. I swam into her and we fucked, so slow I could have fainted. She turned over and lay on her back on me; I was in her from behind and had my hand on her cunt from above as if it were my own, my arm holding her.

And then under the hum and murmur of breathing I heard the soft thump of the man's foot against the closed lower half of the shutter. Fingers gripped the edge and a head floated in silhouette, fuzzy against the glimmer of the garden. My skin opened to welcome him.

THE LIFE OF ART

MY FRIEND AND I went walking the dog in the cemetery. It was a Melbourne autumn: mild breezes, soft air, gentle sun. The dog trotted in front of us between the graves. I had a pair of scissors in my pocket in case we came across a rose bush on a forgotten tomb.

'I don't like roses,' said my friend. 'I despise them for having thorns.'

The dog entered a patch of ivy and posed there. We pranced past the Elvis Presley memorial.

'What would you like to have written on your grave,' said my friend, 'as a tribute?'

I thought for a long time. Then I said, '*Owner of two hundred pairs of boots.*'

When we had recovered, my friend pointed out a headstone which said, *She lived only for others.* 'Poor thing,' said my friend. 'On *my* grave I want you to write, *She lived only for herself.*'

We went stumbling along the overgrown paths.

~

My friend and I had known each other for twenty years, but we had never lived in the same house. She came back from Europe at the perfect moment to take over a room in the house I rented. It became empty because the man— but that's another story.

~

My friend has certain beliefs which I have always secretly categorised as *batty.* Sometimes I have thought, 'My friend is what used to be called "a dizzy dame".' My friend believes in reincarnation: not that this in itself is unacceptable to me. Sometimes she would write me long letters from wherever she was in the world, letters in her lovely, graceful, sweeping hand, full of tales from one or other of her previous lives, tales to explain her psychological make-up and behaviour in her present incarnation. My eye would fly along the lines, sped by embarrassment.

~

My friend is a painter.

~

When I first met my friend she was engaged. She was wearing an antique sapphire ring and Italian boots. Next time I saw her, in Myers, her hand was bare. I never asked. We were students then. We went dancing in a club in South Yarra. The boys in the band were students too. We fancied them, but at twenty-two we felt ourselves to be older women, already fading, almost predatory. We read *The Roman Spring of Mrs Stone*. This was in 1965; before feminism.

~

My friend came off the plane with her suitcase. 'Have you ever noticed,' she said, 'how Australian men, even in their forties, dress like small boys? They wear shorts and thongs and little stripy T-shirts.'

~

A cat was asleep under a bush in our backyard each morning when we opened the door. We took him in. My friend and I fought over whose lap he would lie in while we watched TV.

~

My friend is tone deaf. But she once sang *Blue Moon*, verses and chorus, in a talking, tuneless voice in the back of the car going up the Punt Road hill and down again and over the river, travelling north; and she did not care.

~

My friend lived as a student in a house near the university. Her bed was right under the window in the front room downstairs. One afternoon her father came to visit. He tapped on the door. When no one answered he looked through the window. What he saw caused him to stagger back into the fence. It was a kind of heart attack, my friend said.

~

My friend went walking in the afternoons near our house. She came out of lanes behind armfuls of greenery. She found vases in my dusty cupboards. The arrangements she made with the leaves were stylish and generous-handed.

~

Before either of us married, I went to my friend's house to help her paint the bathroom. The paint was orange, and so was the cotton dress I was wearing. She laughed because all she could see of me when I stood in the bathroom were my limbs and my head. Later, when it got dark, we sat at her kitchen table and she rolled a joint. It was the first dope I had ever seen or smoked. I was afraid that a detective might look through the kitchen window. I could not understand why my friend did not pull the curtain across. We walked up to Genevieve in the warm night and ate two bowls of spaghetti. It seemed to me that I could feel every strand.

~

My friend's father died when she was in a distant country.

'So now,' she said to me, 'I know what grief is.'

'What is it?' I said.

'Sometimes,' said my friend, 'it is what you expect. And sometimes it is nothing more than bad temper.'

When my friend's father died, his affairs were not in order and he had no money.

~

My friend was the first person I ever saw break the taboo against wearing striped and floral patterns together. She stood on the steps of the Shrine of Remembrance and held a black umbrella over her head. This was in the 1960s.

~

My friend came back from Europe and found a job. On the days when she was not painting theatre sets for money she went to her cold and dirty studio in the city and painted for the other thing, whatever that is. She wore cheap shoes and pinned her hair into a roll on her neck.

~

My friend babysat, as a student, for a well-known woman in her forties who worked at night.

'What is she like?' I said.

'She took me upstairs,' said my friend, 'and showed me her bedroom. It was full of flowers. We stood at the door looking in. She said, "Sex is not a problem for me."'

~

When the person…the man whose room my friend had taken came to dinner, my friend and he would talk for hours after everyone else had left the table about different modes of perception and understanding. My friend spoke slowly, in long, convoluted sentences and mixed metaphors, and often laughed. The man, a scientist, spoke in a light, rapid voice, but he sat still. They seemed to listen to each other.

'I don't mean a god in the Christian sense,' said my friend.

'It is egotism,' said the man, 'that makes people want their lives to have meaning beyond themselves.'

~

My friend and I worked one summer in the men's underwear department of a big store in Footscray. We wore our little cotton dresses, our blue sandals. We were happy there, selling, wrapping, running up and down the ladder, dinging the register, going to the park for lunch with the boys from the shop. *I* was happy. The youngest boy looked at us and sighed and said, 'I don't know which one of youse I love the most.' One day my friend was serving a thin-faced woman at the specials box. There was a cry. I looked up. My friend was dashing for the door. She was sobbing. We all stood still, in attitudes of drama. The woman spread her hands. She spoke to the frozen shop at large.

'I never said a thing,' she said. 'It's got nothing to do with *me*.'

I left my customer and ran after my friend. She was halfway down the street, looking in a shop window. She had stopped crying. She began to tell me about… but it doesn't matter now. This was in the 1960s; before feminism.

~

My friend came home from her studio some nights in a calm bliss. 'What we need in work,' she said, 'are those moments of abandon, when the real stuff runs down our arm without obstruction.'

~

My friend cut lemons into chunks and dropped them into the water jug when there was no money for wine.

~

My friend came out of the surgery. I ran to take her arm but she pushed past me and bent over the gutter. I gave her my hanky. Through the open sides of the tram the summer wind blew freely. We stood up and held on to the leather straps. 'I can't sit down,' said my friend. 'He put a great bolt of gauze up me.' This was in the 1960s; before feminism. The tram rolled past the deep gardens. My friend was smiling.

~

My friend and her husband came to visit me and my husband. We heard their car and looked out the upstairs window. We could hear his voice haranguing her, and hers raised in sobs and wails. I ran down to open the door. They were standing on the mat, looking ordinary. We went to Royal Park and flew a kite that her husband had made. The nickname he had for her was one he had picked up from her father. They both loved her, of course. This was in the 1960s.

~

My friend was lonely.

~

My friend sold some of her paintings. I went to look at them in her studio before they were taken away. The smell of the oil paint was a shock to me: a smell I would have thought of as masculine. This was in the 1980s; after feminism. The paintings were big. I did not 'understand' them; but then again perhaps I did, for they made me feel like fainting, her weird plants and creatures streaming back towards a source of irresistible yellow light.

~

'When happiness comes,' said my friend, 'it's so thick and smooth and uneventful, it's like nothing at all.'

~

My friend picked up a fresh chicken at the market. 'Oh,' she said. 'Feel this.' I took it from her. Its flesh was pimpled and tender, and moved on its bones like the flesh of a very young baby.

~

I went into my friend's room while she was out. On the wall was stuck a sheet of paper on which she had written: 'Henry James to a friend in trouble: "throw yourself on the *alternative* life…which is what I mean by the life of art, and which religiously invoked and handsomely understood, je vous le garantis, never fails the sincere invoker—sees him through everything, and reveals to him the secrets of and for doing so."'

~

I was sick. My friend served me pretty snacks at sensitive intervals. I sat up on my pillows and strummed softly the five chords I had learnt on my ukulele. My friend sat on the edge of a chair, with her bony hands folded round a cup, and talked. She uttered great streams of words. Her gaze skimmed my shoulder and vanished into the clouds outside the window. She was like a machine made to talk on and on forever. She talked about how much money she would have to spend on paint and stretchers, about the lightness, the optimism, the femaleness of her work, about what she was going to paint next, about how much tougher and more violent her pictures would have to be in order to attract proper attention from critics, about what the men in her field were doing now, about how she must find this out before she began her next lot of pictures.

'Listen,' I said. 'You don't have to think about any of that. Your work is *terrific*.'

'My work is terrific,' said my friend on a high note, 'but *I'm not*.' Her mouth fell down her chin and opened. She began to sob. 'I'm forty,' said my friend, 'and I've got *no money*.'

I played the chords G, A and C.

'I'm lonely,' said my friend. Tears were running down her cheeks. Her mouth was too low in her face. 'I want a man.'

'You could have one,' I said.

'I don't want just any man,' said my friend. 'And I don't want a boy. I want a man who's not going to think my ideas are crazy. I want a man who'll see the part of me that no one ever sees. I want a man who'll look after me and love me. I want a grown-up.'

I thought, if I could play better, I could turn what she has just said into a song.

'Women like us,' I said to my friend, 'don't have men like that. Why should *you* expect to find a man like that?'

'Why shouldn't I?' said my friend.

'Because men won't do those things for women like us. We've done something to ourselves so that men won't do it. Well—there are men who will. But we despise them.'

My friend stopped crying.

I played the ukulele. My friend drank from the cup.

ALL THOSE BLOODY
YOUNG CATHOLICS

WATTO! ME OLD darling. Where have you been. Haven't seen you since…Let me buy you a drink. Who's your mate? Jan. Goodday Jan. What'll it be, girls? Gin and tonic, yeah. Lemon squash. Fuckin'—well, if that's what you. Hey mate. Mate. Reluctant barmen round here. Mate. Over here. A gin and bloody nonsense, a scotch and water for myself, and a—Jesus Mary and Joseph—*lemon squash*. I know. I asked her but that's what she wanted. Well and how's the world been treating you Watto me old mate. No, not a blue. I was down the Yarra last week in the heat, dived in and hit a snag. Gerry? Still in Perth.

I saw him not so long ago, still a young pup, still a young man, a young Apollo, a mere slip of a lad. I went over to Perth. I always wanted to go over. I've been everywhere of course in Australia, hate to hear those young shits telling me about overseas, what's wrong with here? anyway what? yeah well I've got this mate who's the secretary of the bloody Waterside Workers, right? I says to him, think I'll slip over to Perth. He says, Why don't you go on a boat? I says, What? How much? Don't shit me, he says. For you—nothin'. Was I seasick? On the Bight? No fear. Can't be seasick when you're as drunk as. Can't be the two at the same time. All those seamen drunk, playin' cards, tellin' lies—great trip, I tell you, great trip. Course I got off at the other end had a bit of trouble, once you're back on dry land the booze makes itself felt, but anyway there I was. Yeah yeah, I'm gettin' to Gerry. Blokes on the boat asked me where I was goin', I says, Don't worry, I've got this mate, he works at the university—I didn't tell 'em he was a bloody senior—what is it? senior lecturer? Reader. Anyway first bloke I run into was this other mate, Jimmy Clancy, you'd remember him I suppose, wouldn't like him, bi-i-ig strong bloke, black beard, the lot, always after the women, well he hasn't changed, still running after 'em, I told him off, I lectured him for an hour. Anyway it was great to see him again.

He used to hang round with Laurie Driscoll, Barney O'Brien, Vincent Carroll, Paddy Sheehan, *you* know. Paddy Sheehan? Pad hasn't had a drink in—ooh, must be eight years. He was hittin' it before, though. Tell you about Pad. I was in Sydney not so long ago, went up for the fight, well, on the way home I went through Canberra and I tell you it was shockin'. Yeah I said *shockin'*. Ended up in a sort of home for derelicts—the Home for Homeless Men! Well, I come to out there, I had plenty of money see, it was the fight, the time Fammo beat Whatsisname up Sydney, I had tons of money, tons of it, I says to this Christian bloke out there—he wasn't one of those rotten Christians, he was one of the ones with heart—I says to him, Listen mate, I don't want to stay here, I've got plenty of money, just get me out of here—I've got this mate Paddy Sheehan who's a government secretary or something, so the bloke comes out to pick me up in a bloody chauffeur-driven car, bloke in front with a peaked cap and that, Paddy with his little white freckly face sitting up in the back in his glory—he really laid it on for me. So I says goodbye to the Christian bloke, I says Here, have some of this and I give him some money. How much? Oh I dunno, I had handfuls of it, it was stickin' out of me pockets, I just passed him a handful of notes and away I went in the big black car. All right all right, I'm gettin' to Gerry. Perth wasn't I. Yeah well we sat and we talked of the times that are gone, with all the good people of Perth looking on. Ha ha! Course we did. He's still a boy, full of charm, like a son to me. He was a young tough buck then, love, all handsome and soft, wet behind the ears, and Watto here done the dirty on him, didn't you Watto! Yes you did, you broke his heart, and he was only a boy, yes sweetheart—what was your name again? Watto here she hates me to tell this story, yes she does! He was only a child, straight out of a priestery—no, must have been a monkery because he said he had to wear sandals— course he'd never fucked in his life! Didn't know what to do with his prick! And Watto here goes through him like a packet of salts! Makes mincemeat out of him! Poor bloke never knew what hit him. Drove us all crazy with his bloody guitar playing. She told him didn't you Watto that she didn't want no bloody husband but he wouldn't listen, he was besotted, drawin' her pictures, readin' her the poems of W. B. Yeats, playin' his flamin' guitar—they used to fuck all day and all night, I swear to you love—no shutup Watto! it's true isn't it! I dunno what the other young Catholics in the house thought was goin' on in there—but one day I gets this lettuce and I opens their door a crack and I shoves the lettuce through and I yells out, If you fuck like rabbits you better eat like 'em too!

He he! Look at her blush! Ah Watto weren't they great times. Drinkin' and singin' and fightin' over politics. I remember a party at Mary Maloney's place when Laurie Driscoll spewed in the backyard and passed out—next morning at home he wakes up without his false teeth—he had to call poor Mary and get her to go out in the garden and poke around and see if he hadn't left his teeth behind as well as the contents of his guts. Oh, all those bloody young Catholics—'cept for Gerry, who was corrupted by Watto here—don't get me wrong Wats! you done him a favour—they were all as pure as the driven snow—dyin' of lust but hangin' on like grim death for marriage, ha ha! They thought they were a fire-eatin' mob in those days but they're all good family men now. Course, *I* was never allowed to bring no women home, bloody Barney he tells me, Don't you dare bring those hooers of yours back here, you old dero—I had to sneak them round the lane and into me loft out the back. And finally Watto here gives young Gerald the khyber, he moons tragically for weeks till we're all half crazy—and then he met Christine. *Byoodiful.* Wasn't she Watto. *Byoodiful*…ah…she's still me best mate. Gerry was that keen to impress her the first time he got her to come back to our place, he says to me, Now you stay away, I don't want no foul language, she's a lovely girl. So I stays away and that night I come back

99

real late from the Waiters' Club with this sheila and we're up in the loft and in the morning I didn't know how I was goin' to get her out of there! They were all down in the yard doin' their bloody exercises, Barney and Dell and Derum—so in despair I pushes her out the door of the loft and she misses the ladder and falls down into the yard and breaks both her flamin' legs. Lucky Barney was a final year medical student. Oh Christine was beautiful though—I'll never forget the night you and her brought Gerry back here, Watto, he was that drunk, he'd been found wallowing with his guitar in the flowerbeds outside that girls' dormitory joint you two lived in—youse were draggin' him along between you and he was singin' and laughin' and bein' sick—and then you went off, Watto, and left the poor young girl stranded with this disgusting drunk on her hands! Laugh! Aaahhhhh. Course much later she goes off with Chappo. I remember the night she disappeared. And years after *that* she took off with that show pony McWatsisname, McLaughlin. Didn't you know that? Yeah, she went off with him—course, she's livin' with someone else now. Oh, a beautiful girl. Gorgeous. They fought over her, you know. They fought in the pub, and bloody McLaughlin had a fuckin' aristotle behind his back while poor Chappo had his fists up honourable like this—I got the bottle off McLaughlin.

At least if you blue you should do it proper. Cut it out, I says, look you don't have to fight over cunt! If I was to fight over every sheila I'd ever fucked there'd be fights from here to bloody Darwin! Why do they have to fight over them? Those bloody young Catholics. Gerry. All right all right. And fighting over women! You don't have to *fight* for it! Look if I can't get a fuck there's a thousand bloody massage parlors between here and Sydney, I can go into any one of them and get myself a fuck, without having to *fight* for it. I never put the hard word on you, did I Watto, in all those years? Well, Gerry. Yeah, he was in great form, lovely boy, always felt like a father to him, I taught him everything he knew, I brought him up you might say. Oh, he's been over London and all over the place but he's back over the west now, just the same as ever. Aaaah Watto I've been in love with you for twenty years. Go on. It must be that long. Look at her—turns away and giggles. Well, fifteen then. You're looking in great shape. Gerry. Yeah, yeah…he was a lovely boy. Don't I remember some story about you and him in Perth once? Something about a phone box in the middle of the night? Oh. Right. I'll stop there. Not a word more. You're lookin' in great shape Watto. Your tits are still little though aren't they. How's the baby, my girlfriend? How old is she now? *Nine.* Jeesus Christ. She still goin' to marry me?

I seen her come in here lookin' for your old man one time, he was drinkin' in here with some of the old crowd, she comes in the door there and looks round and spots him. Comes straight up to him and says, Come home! And bugger me if he doesn't down his drink and get up and follow her out the door as meek as a lamb. *Pleeez* sell no more drink to my father / It makes him so strange an' so wild…da da dummm…/ Oh pity the poor drunkard's child. A real little queen. Imagine the kid you and I would have had together eh Watto—one minute swingin' its little fists smashin' everything, next minute mai poetry, mai music, mai drawing! Schizo. Aaah Jesus. Have another drink. You're not going? Ah stay! I only ever see you once every five years. Give us a kiss then. I always did love ya. Ha ha! Don't thank me. Happy New Year and all the best. Ta ta.

A THOUSAND MILES
FROM THE OCEAN

AT KARACHI THEY were not allowed off the plane. She went and stood at the open back door. Everything outside was dust-coloured, and shimmered. Two men in khaki uniforms squatted on the tarmac in the shadow of the plane's tail. They spoke quietly together, with eloquent gestures of the wrists and hands. Behind her, in the cool, the other passengers waited in silence.

The Lufthansa DC10 flew on up the Persian Gulf. Some people were bored and struck up conversations with neighbouring strangers. The Australian beside her opened his briefcase and showed her a plastic album.

It contained photographs of the neon lighting systems he sold. He turned the pages slowly, and told her in detail about each picture. I should never have come. I knew this before I got on the plane. Before I bought the ticket. 'Now this one here,' said the Australian under his moustache, 'is a real goer.' His shoes were pale grey slip-ons with a heel and a very small gold buckle. She found it necessary to keep her eyes off his shoes, which were new, so while she listened she watched another young man, a German, turn and kneel in his seat, lay his arms along the head-rest, and address the person behind him. He looked as if the words he spoke were made of soft, unresisting matter, as if he were chewing air. While she waited for the lavatory she stooped and peered out through a round, distorting window the size of a hubcap. Halfway between her window and the long straight coastline a little white plane, a sheik's plane, spanked along smartly in the opposite direction. If I were on that plane I would be on my way home. I am going the wrong way.

She woke in the hotel. Her watch said 8.30. It was light outside. She went to the window and saw people walking about. The jackhammer stopped. She picked up the phone.

'Excuse me,' she said. 'Is it day or night?'

The receptionist laughed. 'Night,' he said.

She hung up.

In the Hauptbahnhof across the road she bought four oranges, and walked away with them hanging from her hand in a white plastic bag. I will be all right: I can buy. Ich kann kaufen. I should not be here. I can hardly pronounce his name. I am making a very expensive mistake.

In her room she began to dial a number.

On the way up the stairs he kept his hand on the back of her head. He laughed quietly, as if at a private joke.

'I am so tired,' he said. 'I must rest for one hour.'

'I'll read,' she said.

He threw himself face down, straight-legged, fully dressed, on his bed. She wandered away to the white shelves in the hallway. There were hundreds and hundreds of books. The floor was of blond wood laid in a herringbone pattern. The walls were white. The brass doorknobs were polished. The windows were covered with unbleached calico curtains. She took down *Dubliners* and sat at the kitchen table. She sat still. She heard his breathing slow down.

The coffee pot, the strainer, the bread knife still had price stickers on them. In the shelves there were no plates, but several small, odd objects: a green mug with yellow flowers and no handle, a white egg cup with a blue pattern. The kitchen windows opened on to a balcony which was stuffed with empty cardboard cartons stacked inside each other. Beyond the balcony, in someone else's yard, stood a large and leafy tree.

She sat at the table for an hour. Every now and then she turned a page. The sun, which had been shining, went behind a cloud. It did not appear to be any more one season than another.

He came to the kitchen doorway. 'I wish I could have gone to sleep,' he said.

'You were asleep,' she said. 'I heard you breathing.'

Without looking at her he said rapidly, 'I went very deep inside myself.'

She stood up.

'Do you want to see my bicycle?' he said. 'That is mine. Down there.'

'The black one?'

'Ja.'

He stopped the car at a bend in the road. It seemed to be evening but the air was full of light. Flies hovered round the cows' faces. These are the first living creatures, except pigeons and humans, I have seen since I left home.

Frogs creaked. Darkness swam down. They walked. They walked into a wood. While they were passing through it, night came. The paths were wet. Dots of light flickered, went out, rekindled. Under the heavy trees a deer, hip-deep in grass, moved silently away.

They came out of the wood and walked along a road. The road ran beside a body of water. The road was lined with huge trees that touched far overhead. Wind off the water hissed through the trees. Behind them stood high, closed villas with shuttered windows and decorated wooden balconies.

'Beautiful. Beautiful,' he said.

Shutup. On the dark water a pleasure boat passed. Its rails were strung with fairy lights. Broken phrases of music bounced across the cold ripples. Couples danced with their whole fronts touching, out on the deck.

'Is that...the ocean?' she said.

He looked at her, and laughed. 'But we are a souzand *miles* from the ocean!'

They walked by the lake.

'Have you ever had a boat?' she said.

'A boat?'

'Yes.'

'A paddle boat, yes. My father used to take me out in his paddle boat.'

'Do you mean a canoe?' she said. 'A kayak?'

'Something. I hated it. Because my father was a very good...paddler. And he was trying to make me...'

'Tough?'

'Not tough. I was very small and I hated everything. I hated living with my family. I hated my brothers and sisters. He was only trying to make me like something. But I was so small, and sitting in front of this great, strong giant made me feel like a dwarf. And out on the sea—on the lake—he would say "Which way is Peking? Which way is New York?" And I would be so nervous that I couldn't even think. I would guess. And he would say "No!" and hit me, bang, on the head with the paddle.'

There was only one bed. It was narrow. It was his. He sat in the kitchen drinking with his friend. The friend said to her, 'Two main things have changed in this country over the past twenty years. The upbringing of children has become less authoritarian. And there is less militarism.' After midnight, while the two men talked to each other in the kitchen, she undressed and lay on the inside edge of the narrow mattress. At the hotel the sheet on my bed was firmly drawn, and the doona was folded like a wafer at the foot: I paid for comfort, and I got it. She slept till he came to bed, and then it was work all night to keep her back from touching his. Tomorrow I will feel better. Tomorrow I will be less the beaten dog. I will laugh, and be ordinary. His snoring was as loud as the jackhammer. The window was closed tight. Why did he sing to me, at the end of the summer on the other side of the world? Why did he hold me as I was falling asleep and sing me the song about the moon rising? I bled on the sheets and he laughed because the maid was angry. We stood on the cliff edge above an ocean of trees and he borrowed my nail clippers. As he clipped, the tiny sound expanded and rang in the clean air. 'Pik, pik, pik,' he said. Why did he make those phone calls? Why did he cry on the phone in the middle of the night?

He grumbled all the time. He laughed, to pretend it was a joke, but grumbling was his way of talking. Everything was *aw*-ful. His life was *aw*-ful.

'I'm sorry to keep laughing,' she said. 'Why don't you—no.'

'What? What?'

'I keep wanting to make useful suggestions. I know that's annoying.'

'No! No! Zey are good!'

'Why don't you have a massage every week?'

'Who? But who?'

'Why don't you do less of the same work?'

He laughed. 'Zat would be a very bad compromise.'

'You could live on less money, couldn't you?'

He looked distracted. 'But I have to pay for zis *apartment*.'

He went to work and the heavy door closed behind him. She tipped her coffee down the sink. The plughole was blocked by a frill of fried egg white.

She washed herself. She looked at the mirror and away again. She found the key and went down to the courtyard for the bike. An aproned woman on another balcony watched her unchain it, and did not respond to a hand raised in greeting.

The sky was clouded. The seat was high and when she wobbled across an intersection a smoothly pedalling blonde called out, 'Vorsicht!' She stopped and bought a cake of soap and an exercise book with square-ruled pages. She laboured over a map and found her way to a gallery. She passed between its tremendous pillars. It is my duty to look at something. I must drag my ignorance round on my back like a wet coat. He will ask me what I have seen and I must answer. Is there something the matter with me? The paintings look as vulgar as swap-cards, the objects in them as if made of plaster. *Grotte auf Malta 1806:* waves like boiled cauliflower. A heaven full of tumbling pink flabby things. Here is the famous Tintoretto: *Vulkan Überrascht Venus und Mars.* Venus has buds for breasts; a little dog hides under the table. 'The Nazis,' said a Frenchwoman behind her, 'got hold of that Tintoretto and never gave it back.' A small boy lay flat on his stomach on the floor, doing a pencil drawing of an ancient sculpture. His breathing was audible. His pencil made trenches in the paper. His father sat on a bench behind him, waiting and smiling.

In the lavatory she found her pants were black with blood.

The apartment was still empty. It was hard to guess the season or the time of day.

In his apartment there was no broom. There was no iron.

A narrow cupboard full of clothes: the belted raincoat, the Italian jumpers, the dozens of shirts still wrapped from the laundry, each one sporting its little cardboard bow-tie.

A Beethoven violin sonata on the turntable.

Under the bed, a copy of *Don Quixote* and a thermometer.

Through the double-glazed windows passed no sound.

Perhaps he has run away, left town, to get away from me and my unwelcome visit.

On the kitchen wall, a sepia poster of a child, a little girl in romantic gipsy rags, whose glance expressed a precocious sexuality. I am in the wrong country, the wrong town. When I heard the empty hiss of the international call I should have put down the phone. In the middle of his night he took the pills that no longer worked. He cried on the phone. For me, though, it was bright day. I was on the day side of the planet where I had a garden, a house, creatures to care for. I should have hung up the phone. Man muss etwas *machen*, he said, gegen diese Traurigkeit: something has to be *done* about this sadness. Shutup, oh, shutup. Is that the ocean? But we are a souzand *miles* from the ocean!

She walked closer to the furniture. She picked things up and examined them. She went into the cupboard again and pulled a jacket towards her face, then let it drop. That's better. Already making progress.

She went towards the window where his white desk stood. There was a little typewriter on it, and loose heaps of paper, books, envelopes. She twitched the curtain away from a framed picture it was hiding. It was a photo. She took it in her hand. It was herself. A small, dark face, an anxious look. And beneath the photo, under the glass, a torn scrap of paper, non-European paper with horizontal lines instead of squares. Her own handwriting said, *I'm sorry you had to sleep in my blood, but everything else I'm happy about*. She put it back on its hook, dropped the curtain over it, and began to go through the papers.

The apartment was full of letters from women. Barbara, Brigit, Emanuele, Els. Dozens of them. On his work desk. On top of the fridge. In the bedroom. He left the women's letters, single pages of them, scattered round the apartment like little land-mines to surprise himself: under a saucer, between the pages of a book. She read them. Their tone! Dry, clever, working hard at being amusing, at being light. Pathetic. A pathetic tone. Grown women, like herself. 'Capri, c'est pas fini,' wrote one on the back of a postcard. Si, c'est fini. I have spent thousands of dollars to come here and see myself on these pieces of paper. I am now a member of an honourable company.

The telephone began to ring: long, single, European blasts. She dithered. She picked it up. It was not him. It was a young woman. They found a common language and spoke to each other.

'He has my poems,' said the young woman. She was shy, and light-voiced. 'He said that I could call him this weekend. He said we could have a drink together to discuss my poems.'

'I'll take a message.'

'My name is Jeanne. You know? In the French way of writing?'

'I'll tell him, I promise.'

The young woman laughed in her light, nervous voice. 'Thank you. You are very kind.'

Capri, c'est pas fini.

She picked up her bag and went out the door.

At the Hauptbahnhof a ragged dark-haired gipsy woman ran out of a door marked POLIZEI. Her shoes were broken, her teeth were broken. She ran with bent knees and bared teeth. She ran in a curving path across the station and out on to the street. Men looked at each other and laughed.

The train went south. South, and south. It stopped at every station. People got in and people got out. It ran along between mountains whose tops were crisp. People carried parcels and string bags, and sometimes children. They greeted each other in blurred dialects. The train crossed borders, it ran across a whole country. A grandmother ate yogurt out of a plastic jar. She raised and dipped the spoon with a mechanical gesture. She licked the white rim off her lips and swallowed humbly. The train slid through a pass beside a jade river. Tremors rose from the river's depths and shuddered on its swollen surface. After the second border she opened the window. The train passed close to buildings the colour of old flowerpots, buildings set at random angles among dense foliage, buildings whose corners were softened with age. The shutters were green; they were fixed back against the walls to make room for washing and for red geraniums. The air had colour and texture. You could touch the air. It was yellow. It was almost pink. She turned back to the compartment and it was full of the scent of sleeping children.

DID HE PAY?

HE PLAYED GUITAR. You could see him if you went to dance after midnight at Hides or Bananas, horrible mandrax dives where no one could steer a straight course, where a line of supplicants for the no-cost miracle, accorded to some, waited outside the door, gazing through the slats of the trellis at his shining head. Closer in, they saw him veiled in an ethereal mist of silvery-blue light and cigarette smoke, dressed in a cast-off woman's shirt and walked-on jeans, his glasses flashing round panes of blankness as they caught the light, his blond hair matted into curls: an angel stretched tight, grimacing with white teeth and anguished smiles. In the magic lights, that's how he looked.

He was a low-lifer who read political papers, and who sometimes went home, or to what had once been home, to his fierce wife who ran their child with the dull cries of her rage and who played bass herself, thumping the heart rhythm, learning her own music to set herself free of his. They said she was rocking steady.

'To papa from child' wrote the little girl on his birthday card. She was a nuggety kid with cowlicks of blond hair, a stubborn lower lip and a foghorn voice. Her parents were engaged in their respective and mutual struggles, and imperiously she demanded the bodies and arms of other grown-ups, some of whom recoiled in fear before the urgency of her need. A performers' child, she knew she existed. She knew the words of every song that both her parents' bands played. You'd hear her crooning them in the huge rough backyard where the dope plants grew, chuckling in her husky voice at the variations she invented:

'Don't you know what love is? Don't you love your nose?'

'Call me papa!' he shouted in the kitchen.

'Papa! Papa!' she cried, thumping joyfully round him on her stumpy legs. Having aroused this delight he

turned away, forgot her, picked up his guitar and went
to work. The child wept loudly with her nose snotting
down her face: like her mother, she was accustomed to
the rage of rejection and knew no restraint in its expression. In her room she made a dressing-table out of an
upturned cardboard carton covered with a cloth. She
lined up a brush, a comb and an old tube of lipstick upon
it.

The parents had met in a car-park in a satellite
town, where kids used to hang out. Everyone wondered
how they'd managed to stay together that long, given his
lackadaisical ways and her by now chronic anger. The
women knew her rage was just, but she frightened even
the feminists with her handsome, sad monkey's face and
furious straight brows. It was said that once she harangued
him from the audience when he was on stage at one of the
bigger hotels. Somehow it was clear that they were tied
to each other. Both had come from another country, as
children. 'When he's not around I just…miss him,' she
said to her friend. It cost her plenty to say this.

'Old horse-face,' he called himself once, when they
ran an unflattering photo of him in the daily paper, bent
like licorice to the microphone, weighed down by the
heavy white Gibson, spectacles hiding from the viewer
all but his watchful corner-smile. He was sickeningly

thin; his legs and hips were thin past the point of permission. In spite of guitar muscles, his finger and thumb could meet round his upper arm. One of the women asked him why he was doing this, in bed one morning. 'Finger-lengthening exercises,' he said, and she didn't even laugh.

He was irresistible. His hair was silvery blond, short, not silky but thick, and he had a habit of rubbing the back of his head and grinning like a hick farmer, as if at his own fecklessness. He would hold your gaze a second longer than was socially necessary, as if promising an alliance, an unusual intimacy. When he smiled, he turned his mouth down at the corners, and when he sang, his mouth stretched as if in agony; or was it a smile? It did for women, whatever it was. Some people, if they had got around to talking about it, might have said that there was something in his voice that would explain everything, if you could only listen hard enough: maybe he had a cold; or maybe he did what everyone wants a musician to do— cry for you, because you have lost the knack.

Winter was a bad time in that town. Streets got longer and greyer, and it was simply not possible to manage without some sort of warmth. He was pathetic with money, and unable to organise a house for himself when his wife wouldn't have him any longer. Yes, she broke it. Not only did she give him the push: she installed another man, and told her husband that if he wasn't prepared to be there when he said he would, he could leave the child alone. He ground his teeth that day. He hadn't known he would run out of track, but he knew enough to realise he had no right to be angry. He walked around all afternoon, in and out of kitchens, unable to say what the matter was. He couldn't sit still.

After that he drifted from house to house between gigs, living on his charm: probably out of shame rather than deviousness, he never actually asked for anything. Cynics may say his technique was more refined: pride sometimes begets tenderness, against people's will. He just hung around, anyway, till someone offered, or until it eventuated with the passing of time: a meal, a place to sleep, a person to sleep with. If someone he was not interested in asked him to spend the night with her, he was too embarrassed to say no. Thus, many a woman spent a puzzled night beside him, untouched, unable to touch.

In the households he was never in the way. In fact, he was a treat to have around, with his idle wit and ironic smile, and his bony limbs and sockless ankles, and his way of laughing incredulously, as if surprised that anything could still amuse him. He was dead lazy, he did nothing but accept with grace, a quality rare enough to pave his way for a while at least. If any of the men resented his undisputed sway, his exemption from the domestic criticism to which they themselves were subjected, their carpings were heard impatiently by the women, or dismissed with contempt as if they were motivated only by envy. Certain women, feeling their generosity wearing thin, or reluctantly suspecting that they were being used, suppressed this heresy for fear of losing the odd gift of his company, the illusion of his friendship. Also, it was considered a privilege to have other people see him in your kitchen. He had a big reputation. He was probably the best in town.

After his late gigs he was perfect company for people who watched television all night, warmed by the blue glow and the hours of acquiescence. The machine removed from him the necessity of finding a bed. The other person would keep the fire alight all through the night, going out every few hours to the cold shed where the briquettes were kept, lugging the carton in and piling the dusty black blocks on to the flames. He would flick the channel over.

'That'll do,' she'd say, whoever she was.

'No. That's *War and Peace*. No. Let's watch *Cop Shop*. That's all right, actually. That's funny.'

It wasn't really his fault that people fell in love with him. He was so passive that anyone could project a fantasy on to him, and so constitutionally pleasant that she could well imagine it reciprocated. His passivity engulfed women. They floundered in it helplessly. Surely that downward smile meant something? It wasn't that he didn't *like* them, he merely floated, apparently without will in the matter.

It was around this time that he began to notice an unpleasant phenomenon. When he brought his face close to a woman's, to kiss, he experienced a slow run of giddiness, and her face would dwindle inexorably to the size of a head viewed down the wrong end of a telescope, or from the bottom of a well. It was disagreeable to the point of nausea.

All the while he kept turning out the songs. His bands, which always burnt out quickly on the eve of success, played music that was both violent and reasonable. His guitar flew sometimes, worked by those bony fingers. He did work, then? It could be said that he worked to give something in exchange for what he took, were this not such a hackneyed rationalisation of the vanity and selfishness of musicians; let us divest him of such honourable intent, and say rather that what he played could be accepted in payment by those who felt that something was

127

due. He could play so that the blood moved in your veins. You could accept and move; or jack up on him. It was all the same to him, in the end.

He worked at clearing the knotty channels, at re-aligning his hands and his imagination so harmoniously that no petty surge of wilfulness could obstruct the strong, logical stream. It was hard, and most often he failed, but once in a while he touched something in himself that was pure. He believed that most people neither noticed nor cared, that the music was noise that shook them up and covered them while they did what they had come for. Afterwards he would feel emptied, dizzy with unconsumed excitement, and very lonely.

Sometimes guitar playing became just a job with long blank spaces which he plugged with dope and what he called romance, a combination which blurred his clarity and turned him soggy. In Adelaide he met a girl who came to hear the band and took him home, not before he had kept her waiting an hour and a half in the band room while he exchanged professional wise-cracks with the other musicians. In the light that came in stripes through her Venetian blinds she revealed that she loved to kiss. He didn't want to, he couldn't. 'Don't maul me,' he said. She was too young and too nice to be offended. She even thought he liked her. Any woman was better than three-to-a-room motel nights with the band. He was always longing for something.

A woman came to the motel with some sticks for the band. She had red henna'd hair, a silver tooth earring, a leopard skin sash, black vinyl pants. She only stayed a minute, to deliver. When she left, he was filled with loss. He smoked and read all night.

When the winter tour was over, he came south again. He called the girl he thought had been in love with him before he went away.

'I don't want to see you,' she said. 'Have a nice band, or something.'

She hung up. At his next gig he saw this girl in the company of his wife. They stood well back, just in front of the silent, motionless row of men with glasses in their hands. They did not dance, or talk to each other, or make a move to approach him between sets, but it was obvious that they were at ease in each other's company. He couldn't help seeking out their two heads as he played. Late in the night, he turned aside for a second to flick his lead clear of an obstruction, and when he looked back, the women were gone.

When he got to the house the front was dark, but he could see light coming from the kitchen at the back. He knocked. Someone walked quickly up the corridor to the door and opened it. It was not his wife, but the girl. He made as if to enter, but she fronted her body into the doorway and said in a friendly voice, 'Look—why don't you just piss off? You only make people miserable. It's easier if you stay away.'

The kitchen door at the other end of the hall became a yellow oblong standing on end with a cut-out of his wife's head, sideways, pasted on to it halfway down.

'Who is it?' she called out. He heard the faint clip of the old accent.

'No one,' shouted the girl over her shoulder, and shut the door quietly in his face. He heard her run back down the corridor on her spiky heels. He thought she was laughing. Moll.

That night he dreamed: as the train moved off from the siding, he seized the handrail and swung himself up on to the step. Maliciously it gathered speed: the metal thing hated him and was working to shake him off. He hung on to the greasy rail and tried to force the van door open, but the train had plunged into a mine, and was turning on sickening angles so that he could not get his balance. There was roaring and screeching all around, and a dank smell. Desperately he clung, half off the step, his passport pressed between his palm and the handrail.

The train heeled recklessly on to the opposite track and as he fought for balance the passport whisked away and was gone, somewhere out in the darkness. Beneath the step he saw the metal slats of a bridge flash by, and oily water a long way down. He threw back his head and stretched open his mouth, but his lungs cracked before he could utter a sound.

The band folded. He might get used to it, but he would never learn to like the loosened chest and stomach muscles, the vague desolation, the absence where there ought to have been the nightly chance to match himself against his own disorder and the apathy of white faces. He got a job, on the strength of his name and what he knew about music, doing a breakfast show on FM radio. You could hear him every morning, supposed to start at seven thirty on the knocker, but often you'd roll over at twenty to and flick on the transistor and hear nothing but the low buzz of no one there. Lie back long enough and you'd hear the click, the hum and at last his voice, breathless but not flustered.

'Morning, listeners. Bit late starting. Sorry. Here's the Flaming Groovies.'

He had nowhere much to sleep, now, so different women knew the stories behind these late starts. Shooting smack, which he had once enjoyed, only made him spew.

One night when nothing turned up he slept on the orange vinyl couch at the studio. The traffic noise woke him, and at seven thirty he put on a record, and chewed up a dried-out chocolate eclair and some Throaties. He thought he was going to vomit on air.

With the radio money, dearly earned by someone with his ingrained habit of daylight sleeping, he took a room in a house beside a suburban railway station. There was nothing in the room. He bought a mattress at the Brotherhood, and borrowed a blanket. He shed his few clothes and lay there with his face over the edge of the mattress, almost touching the lino. In the corner stood his Gibson in its rigid case. He dozed, and dreamed that the drummer from his old band took him aside and played him a record of something he called 'revolutionary music', music the likes of which he had never heard in his life, before the sweetness and ferocity of which his own voice died, his instrument went dumb, his fingers turned stiff and gummy. He woke up weeping, and could not remember why.

The girl who kissed arrived from Adelaide one Saturday morning, unheralded. She invaded the room with her niceness and her cleanliness and the expectation that they would share things. That night he stayed away, lounged in kitchens, drifted till dawn, and finally lent himself to a woman with dyed blond hair and a turn of phrase that made him laugh. When he went back the next night, the kisser had gone.

There were no curtains in the room, and the window was huge. He watched the street and the station platform for hours at a time, leaning lightly against the glass. People never looked up, which was just as well, for he was only perving. At five thirty every morning a thunderous diesel express went by and woke him. It was already light: summer was coming. He supposed that there were questions which might be considered, and answered. He didn't try to find out. He just hung on.

CIVILISATION AND
ITS DISCONTENTS

PHILIP CAME. I went to his hotel: I couldn't get there fast enough. He stepped up to me when I came through the door, and took hold of me.

'Hullo,' he said, 'my dear.'

People here don't talk like that. My hair was still damp.

'Did you drive?' he said.

'No. I came on the bus.'

'The *bus*?'

'There's never anywhere to park in the city.'

'You've had your hair cut. You look like a boy.'

'I know. I do it on purpose. I dress like a boy and I have my hair cut like a boy. I want to *be* a boy. So I can have a homosexual affair with *you*.'

He laughed. 'Good girl!' he said. At these words I was so flooded with well-being that I could hardly get my breath. 'If you were a boy some of the time and a girl the rest,' he said, 'I'd be luckier. Because I could have both.'

'No,' I said. 'I'd be luckier. Because I could *be* both.'

I scrambled out of my clothes.

'You're so thin,' he said.

'I don't eat. I'm sick.'

'Sick? Are you?' He put his two hands on my shoulders and looked into my eyes like a doctor.

'Sick with love.'

'Your eyes are healthy. Lustrous. Are mine?'

His room was on the top floor. Opposite, past some roofs and a deep street, was the old-fashioned tower of the building in which a dentist I used to go to had his rooms. That dentist was so gentle with the drill that I never needed an injection. I used to breathe slowly, as I had been taught at yoga: the pain was brief. I didn't flinch. But he made his pile and moved to Queensland.

The building had a flagpole. Philip and I stood at the window with no clothes on and looked out. The tinted glass made the cloud masses more detailed, richer, more spectacular than they were.

'Look at those,' I said. 'Real boilers. Coming in from somewhere.'

'Just passing through,' said Philip. He was looking at the building with the tower. 'I love the Australian flag,' he said. 'Every time I see it I get a shiver.'

'I'm like that about the map.' Once I worked in a convent school in East London. I used to go to the library at lunchtime, when the nuns were locked away in their dining room being read to, and take down the atlas and gaze at the page with Australia on it: I loved its upper points, its vast inlets, its fat sides, the might of it, the mass from whose south-eastern corner my small life had sprung. I used to crouch between the stacks and rest the heavy book on the edge of the shelf: I could hardly support its weight. I looked at the map and my eyes filled with tears.

'Did I tell you she's talking about coming back to me?' said Philip.

'Do you want her to?'

'Of course I do.'

I sat down on the bed.

'We'll have to start behaving like adults,' he said. 'Any idea how it's done?'

'Well,' I said, 'it must be a matter of transformation. We have to turn what's happening now into something else.'

'You sound experienced.'

'I am.'

'What can we turn it into?'

'Brother and sister? A lifelong friendship?'

'Oh,' he said, 'I don't know anything about that. Can't people just go on having a secret affair?'

'I don't like lying.'

'You don't have to. I'm the liar.'

'What makes you so sure she won't find out? People always know. She'll take one look at you and know. That's what wives are for.'

'We'll see.'

'How can you stand it?' I said. 'It's dishonourable. How can you lie to someone and still love her?'

'Forced to. Forced by love to be a hypocrite.'

I thought for a second he was joking.

'We could drop it now,' I said.

'What are you *saying*?'

'I don't mean it.'

Not yet. The sheets in those hotels are silky, but crisp. How do they get them like that? A lot of starch, and ironing, things no housewife in her right mind could be bothered doing. The bed was wide enough for another two people to have lain in it, and still none of us would have had to touch sides. I don't usually go to bed in the daylight. And as if the daylight were not enough, the room was full of lamps. I started to switch them off, one after another, and thinking of the phrase 'full of lamps' I remembered something my husband said to me, long after we split up, about a Shakespearean medley he had seen performed by doddering remnants of a famous British company that was touring Australia. 'The stage,' he said, 'was covered in *thrones*,' and his knees bent with laughter. He was the only man I have ever known who would rejoice with you over the petty triumphs of the day. I got under the sheet. I couldn't help laughing to myself, but it was too complicated to explain why.

Philip had a way of holding me, when we lay down: he made small rocking movements, so small that I sometimes wondered if I were imagining them, if the comfort of being held were translating itself into an imaginary cradling.

'I've never told anyone I loved them, before,' said Philip.

'Don't be silly,' I said.

'You don't know anything about me.'

'At your age?' I said. 'A married man? You've never loved anyone before?'

'I've never *said* it before.'

'No wonder she went away,' I said. 'Men are really done over, aren't they. At an early age.'

'Why do you want to fuck like a boy, then?'

'Just for play.'

'Is it allowed?' he said.

'Who by?' I said. I was trying to be smart; but seriously, who says we can't? Isn't that why women and men make love? To bend the bars a little, just for a little; to let the bars dissolve? Philip pinched me. He took hold of the points of my breasts, between forefingers and thumbs. I could see his teeth. He pinched hard. It hurt. I liked it. And he bit me. He *bit* me. When I got home I looked in the mirror and my shoulders and arms were covered in small round bruises.

I went to his house, in the town where he lived. I told him I would be passing through on my way south, and he invited me, and I went, though I had plenty of friends I could have stayed with in that city.

There was a scandal in the papers as I passed through the airport that evening, about a woman who had made a contract to have a baby for a childless couple. The baby was born, she changed her mind, she would not give it up. Everyone was talking about her story.

I felt terrible at his house, for all I loved him, with his wife's forgotten dressing-gown hanging behind the door like a witness. I couldn't fall asleep properly. I 'lay broad waking' all night long, and the house was pierced by noises, as if its walls were too flimsy to protect it from the street: a woman's shoes striking the pavement, a gate clicking, a key sliding into a lock, stairs breathing in and out. It never gets truly dark in cities. Once I rolled over and looked at him. His face was sleeping, serene, smiling on the pillow next to mine like a cherub on a cloud.

He woke with a bright face. 'I feel unblemished,' he said, 'when I've been with you.' This is why I loved him, of course: because he talked like that, using words and phrases that most people wouldn't think of saying. 'When I'm with you,' he'd say, 'I feel happy and free.'

He made the breakfast and we read the papers in the garden.

'She should've stuck to her word,' he said.

'Poor thing,' I said. 'How can anyone give a baby away?'

'But she promised. What about the couple? They must be dying to have a kid.'

'Are you?'

'Yes,' he said, and looked at me with the defiant expression of someone expecting to be crossed. 'Yes. I am.'

The coffee was very strong. It was bad for me in the mornings. It made my heart beat too fast.

'I think in an ideal world everyone would have children,' I said. 'That's how people learn to love. Kids suck love out of your bones.'

'I suppose you think that only mothers know how to love.'

'No. I don't think that.'

'Still,' he said. 'She signed a contract. She *signed*. She made a promise.'

'Philip,' I said, 'have you ever smelled a baby's head?'

The phone started to ring inside the house, in the room I didn't go into because of the big painting of her that was hanging over the stereo. Thinking that he loved me, though I understood and believed I had accepted the futurelessness of it, I amused myself by secretly calling it The Room in Which the First Wife Raved, or Bluebeard's Bloody Chamber: it repelled me with an invisible force, though I stood at times outside its open door and saw its pleasantness, its calm, its white walls and wooden floor on which lay a bent pattern of sunlight like a child's drawing of a window.

He ran inside to answer the phone. He was away for quite a while. I thought about practising: how it is possible to learn with one person how to love, and then to apply the lesson learnt to somebody else: someone teaches you to sing, and then you wait for a part in the right opera. It was warm in the garden. I dozed in my chair. I had a small dream, one of those shockingly vivid dreams that occur when one sleeps at an unaccustomed time of day, or when one ought to be doing something other than sleeping. I dreamed that I was squatting naked with my vagina close to the ground, in the posture we are told primitive women adopt for childbearing ('They just squat down in the fields, drop the baby, and go on working'). But someone was operating on me, using sharp medical instruments on my cunt. Bloody flesh was issuing from it in clumps and clots. I could watch it, and see it, as if it were somebody else's cunt, while at the same time experiencing it being done to me. It was not painful. It didn't hurt at all.

I woke up as he came down the steps smiling. He crouched down in front of me, between my knees, and spoke right into my face.

'You want me to behave like a married man, and have kids, don't you?'

'*Want* you to?'

'I mean you think I should. You think everyone should, you said.'

'Sure—if that's what you want. Why?'

'Well, on the phone just now I went a bit further towards it.'

'You mean you *lined* it *up*?'

'Not exactly—but that's the direction I'm going in.'

I looked down at him. His forearms were resting across my knees and he was crouching lightly on the balls of his feet. He was smiling at me, smiling right into my eyes. He was waiting for me to say, *Good boy!*

'Say something reassuring,' he said. 'Say something close, before I go.'

I took a breath, but already he was not listening. He was ready to work. Philip loved his work. He took on more than he could comfortably handle. Every evening he came home with his pockets sprouting contracts. He never wasted anything: I'd hear him whistling in the car, a tiny phrase, a little run of notes climbing and falling as we drove across the bridges, and then next morning from the room with the synthesiser in it would issue the same phrase but bigger, fuller, linked with other ideas, becoming a song: and a couple of months after that I'd hear it through the open doors of every café, record shop and idling car in town. 'Know what I used to dream?' he said to me once. 'I used to dream that when I pulled up at the lights I'd look into the cars on either side of me and in front and behind, and everyone would be singing along with the radio, and they'd all be singing the same song. Even if the windows were wound up we'd read each other's lips, and everyone would laugh, and wave.'

I made my own long distance call. 'I'll be home tonight, Matty,' I said.

His voice was full of sleep. 'They rang up from the shop,' he said. 'I told them you were sick. Have you seen that man yet?'

'Yes. I'm on my way. Get rid of the pizza boxes.'

'I need money, Mum.'

'When I get there.'

Philip took me to the airport. I was afraid someone would see us, someone he knew. For me it didn't matter. Nothing was secret, I had no one to hide anything from, and I would have been proud to be seen with him. But for him I was worried. I worried enough for both of us. I kept my head down. He laughed. He would not let me go. He tried to make me lift my chin; he gave it soft butts with his forehead. My cheeks were red.

'I'm always getting on planes with tears in my eyes,' I said.

'They'll be getting to know you,' he said. 'Are you too

shy to kiss me properly?'

I bolted past the check-in desk. I looked back and he was watching me, still laughing, standing by himself on the shining floor.

On the plane I was careful with myself. I concentrated on the ingenuity of the food tray, its ability to remain undisturbed by the alterations in position of the seatback to which it was attached. I called for a scotch and drank it. My mistake was to look inside a book of poems, the only reading matter I had on me. They were poems so charged with sex and death and longing that it was indecent to read them in public: I was afraid that their power might leak out and scandalise the onlookers. I kept the book turned away from two men who were sitting between me and the window. They were drinking German beer and talking in a European language of which I did not recognise a single word. One of them turned his head and caught my eye. I expected him to look away hastily, for I felt myself to be ugly and stiff with sadness; but his face opened into a dazzling smile.

My son was waiting for the plane. He had come out on the airport bus. He saw how pleased I was, and looked down with an embarrassed smile, but he permitted me to hug him, and patted my shoulder with little rapid pats.

'Your face is different,' he said. 'All sort of emotional.'

'Why do you always pat me when you hug me?'

'Pro'ly 'cause you're nearly always in a state,' he said.

He asked me to wait while he had a quick go on the machines. His fingers swarmed on the buttons. *Death By Acne* was the title of a thriller he had invented to make me laugh: but his face in concentration lost its awkwardness and became beautiful. I leaned on the wall of the terminal and watched the people passing.

A tall young man came by. He was carrying a tiny baby in a sling against his chest. The mother walked behind, smooth-faced and long-haired, holding by the hand a fat-nappied toddler. But the man was the one in love with the baby. He walked slowly, with his arms curved round its small bulk. His head was bowed so he could gaze into its face. His whole being was adoring it.

I watched the young family go by in its peaceful procession, each one moving quietly and contentedly in place, and I heard the high-pitched death wails of the space creatures my son was murdering with his fast and delicate tapping of buttons, and suddenly I remembered walking across the street the day after I brought him home from hospital. The birth was long and I lost my rhythm and made too much noise and they drugged me, and when it was over I felt that now I knew what the prayerbook meant when it said *the pains of death gat hold upon me.*

But crossing the road that day, still sore from knives and needles, I saw a pregnant woman lumbering towards me, a woman in the final stages of waiting, putting one heavy foot in front of the other. Her face as she passed me was as calm and as full as an animal's: 'a face that had not yet received the fist'. And I envied her. I was stabbed, pierced with envy, with longing for what was about to happen to her, for what she was ignorantly about to enter. I could have cried out, Oh, let me do it again! Give me another chance! Let me meet the mighty forces again and struggle with them! Let me be rocked again, let me lie helpless in that huge cradle of pain!

'Another twenty cents down the drain,' said my son. We set out together towards the automatic doors. He was carrying my bag. I wanted to say to him, to someone, 'Listen. Listen. I am *hopelessly in love*.' But I hung on. I knew I had brought it on myself, and I hung on until the spasm passed. And then I began to recreate from memory the contents of the fridge.

MY HARD HEART

'Do you call that soul, that thing
that chirps in you so timorously?'
Rainer Maria Rilke

I MET MY husband at the airport, and there he told me some things that wiped the smile off my face. He put his suitcase down outside the Intercontinental Bar and leant his face and arms on the fire hose: he wept, I did not. We drove home. He lay on the bed and sobbed. I went downstairs and sat beside my daughter on the couch. She was watching a Fred Astaire movie and did not notice how I gazed at the side of her smiling face, as if in that glossy skin I might find meaning.

I lay beside him in the hard bed and listened to him talking, explaining, crying. I said nothing. My limbs and torso swelled. Slowly I ballooned. I became tremendous. I was colossal, a thing that weighed a ton, a bulky immovable slab of clay set cold, baked hard and heartless. Somewhere in the centre of this inert mass was a tiny spark, hardly a spark at all, only barely alight.

In a day he was gone. The smell of the house changed immediately. I got up in the morning and stepped out of my bedroom. The door of his old room, the upstairs one with the balcony, stood open, and across its empty air fell a slice of sunlight.

The front of the house was festooned with great twining loops of wisteria. People walked slowly past, gazing up. A delicate, warm scent puffed out of the dangling flowers, and when I sat on a cushion on the doorstep and played my ukulele I saw that the flower clumps were full of bees.

I knew it was a passing euphoria, but all my senses were working. Crowds parted as I approached, old men and boys and babies smiled at me in the street, waitresses spoke to me with a tender address. When I tried to play, notes placed themselves under my fingers. Milky clouds covered the sky, a warm dry wind blew all day, shocks of perfume came from behind fences. I remembered being a student, the delicious agony of exams in spring.

'You wait,' said Suzie in the wine bar. 'In six weeks

you'll be walking on rocks. You'll have a brick wall six inches in front of your face.'

I bought a Petpak at Ansett and took our cat with me to visit Vanessa in the country. I set him free at the door and he bolted away into what would one day be a garden. Vanessa was wearing sagging purple socks. I sat with her at the kitchen table. She showed me a book by C. G. Jung which contained a series of mandalas painted by one of his patients. The first pictures were grim prisons of rocks and stones, but as the series progressed, oceans appeared and the air inside the circular frames flushed, thinned and became breathable.

'What *is* a mandala, exactly?'

'I don't know,' she said. 'Is it a picture of the soul, at a given moment?'

I pulled a chair over to the big window and sat watching the movements of the long grasses in the wind.

'Will I be walking on rocks?'

Vanessa shrugged. She lives alone in a house which from the outside looks small and square but which encloses, with a light touch, one enormous room on several levels, a space of unusual flexibility. The kitchen is right in the centre: everything else radiates from there.

The cat returned at five in the morning and began to complain and cry. At home I would have thrown him into the kitchen and shut the door, but here, because I was a visitor in the huge room where Vanessa also slept, I had to feed him and bring him on to my bed. When at last he settled down with my hand on his side, I remembered the nights with a new baby: the alarm, the broken sleep, the silently turned doorknob, the plodding from task to task; the despair of fatigue, but the weary patience, and the acceptance of the fact that it is absolutely required of one to do these things: the bearing of duty.

I approached our house in the evening. It was 'lit up from door to top'. I knew there was no one inside it now but my daughter: I felt her tough little spirit burning away inside its many rooms. I cooked a meal and we tried to eat it elegantly, facing each other across the white table-cloth. She put on an old Aretha Franklin record: I had brought her up not to be like the girl in the song, the one who 'don't remember the Queen of Soul'. At those feathery cries we rolled our eyes and gave each other shy smiles. We washed the dishes together. I put my forehead on the windowsill and cried with my hands still in the hot water, and she said, 'I know this is much worse for you than it is for me.'

In the café Elizabeth told me her husband was dying of a tumour.

'I used to think there was justice,' she said, 'and fairness. That there was a contract, that things meant something. Now I know your foot can go straight through the floor.'

'And what's on the other side?'

'Nothing.'

'Nothing?'

'Nothing.'

Tears, black with mascara, poured off her face. She cried in silence, without sobs.

'I think what I'm trying to do,' she said, 'is to die. Because I can't *bear* him to have to go out there on his own.'

I was ashamed of my story when she asked for it, a simple tale of marriage betrayed, but she listened with respect.

'We were bright girls, weren't we,' she said. 'What bright girls we were!'

We kissed goodbye, and sat quietly. I put my hand on her stockinged leg. 'Aren't those boots beautiful,' I said.

We looked at the boots without speaking. In perfect unison we heaved two great sighs.

I saw my husband sitting in the café with a woman we both knew. I went without thinking to the same table: the three of us said good morning and they went on reading the papers. When my husband got up to go to work he nodded to me and said to the other woman, 'I'll pay yours.'

At home I answered the phone. A young woman asked for my husband.

'He's not here,' I said, 'at the moment. This is his wife speaking.' I told her my name.

'Oh yes!' said the young woman. 'He told me he was involved with you.'

'Involved!' I said. 'He's *married* to me.'

'Oh well,' she said with an airy laugh. 'Married… involved…'

I filled the bucket and got the mop out of the yard and began to wash the kitchen floor. The tiles were filthy and I had to scrub; their edges chipped and crumbled in the foam. My daughter came into the room behind me and opened the fridge. She uttered a dramatic cry of pain. I was used to this.

'What happened?' I said, without turning round.

'I hit myself in the *eye*. With the freezer *door*.'

'How'd you manage to do that?' I said, and continued to mop.

She said nothing, and did not move. When I looked around, she was still standing at the closed fridge door with her palms over her eyes. I stripped off the rubber gloves and went to put my arms round her. She was as stiff as a rail.

'Are you all right?'

'Obviously not,' she snapped from behind her hands.

I flinched. 'Oh—don't talk to me like that.'

'You never know!' she burst out. 'You never know how to comfort someone who's hurt themselves! And now I'm the same—I can't either. I've picked it up from *you*.'

I met Steve in the bank. He had driven down from Sydney in a panel van so heavy with carpentry equipment that he parked it under a tree outside my house and went everywhere by tram. He had a very small black bible which he carried in his shirt pocket. I knew his brother, but I didn't know him.

He put his budgie's cage on the highest kitchen cupboard and we watched the cat licking its lips. The budgie perched on my daughter's shoulder while she played the piano, and accompanied her with thrilling inventions.

'Have you ever been married?' I said.

'No,' said Steve. 'But I'm familiar with the pain.'

After dinner we watched an American gospel show on TV: the pastor stood waist-deep in a brown river and dunked the people one by one: up they came, spouting and fighting and babbling in strange tongues. Their faces were distorted, their eyes were closed, their bodies bloated or emaciated. Somebody somewhere was picking at a banjo: that tricky, tough, humble music.

Between the gospel show and *Six Centuries of British Verse* we took the dog out and walked a figure of eight around the enormous park. The night was starry, the air was cool, the big avenues of elms looked low and humped from where we were, in the middle of the football ovals.

'Did you get baptised in a river?' I said. It was a kind of flirtation, but he never bit. He looked at me with his face open, ready to laugh.

'No,' he said. 'At a beach. In the ocean.'

'What happened, exactly?'

'Oh—I don't know if all that detail would be useful to you.'

'Are you trying to be "useful" to me?' I said sharply.

He turned and looked at me. 'You asked me,' he said, 'and I'm trying to answer.'

We walked. The dog heard possums in the trees and sprang helplessly into the air at the base of the thick, ridged trunks. Half a mile away, along the western boundary of the huge park, silent headlights moved in a formal line, as if in convoy to a funeral, or a wedding.

'I haven't slept with anyone for a really long time,' he said. 'For years.'

'You must be absolutely radiant with it,' I said.

He laughed. 'I'm celibate, but I'm not asexual. It's not so bad. It's not bad at all. I was like you. I had a heart of stone. I was all black inside. I was grieving over everything. I'd feel an impending relationship, and I'd know I had nothing to give. So I stopped. In Ezekiel, I think it is, he says, "I will take away your heart of stone, and I will give you a heart of flesh".'

That night the poet on *Six Centuries of British Verse* was Milton. Across the screen stumbled painted Adams and Eves from every era but ours: in various postures denoting shame, humiliation and grief, they staggered into exile.

When the program was finished he stood up and leaned over me, and kissed me on the cheek.

'Good night!' we said. 'Sleep well!'

Upstairs in my room I pulled the curtain open and lay down in a current of night air. The curtain brushed and brushed against the windowsill. I heard a tram go chattering through the intersection, then the street outside was quiet.

The little flame stirred in its cage of clay: I felt it shiver, and begin to move.

THE PSYCHOLOGICAL
EFFECT OF WEARING
STRIPES

HERE IS MY photo of Philip. I took it at the check-in counter. See that bag? His linen jacket's in there, rolled up. That's how he gets it crushed in exactly the right way. He travels a lot, so much that I never know where he is or when he's going to turn up. He likes this photo, or so he said when he rang. 'Thanks,' he said. 'Usually I pose, but this one's really nice. You caught me.' It wasn't hard. I've seen people pose. Cameras are bad enough, but have you ever watched someone you know front their own reflection in a mirror? (I exclude actors, who examine themselves coldly and without vanity, like workers checking their tools.) You see a stiffening, a closing, a dimming; you see them pull on their idea of themselves, the caricature that will soften and melt away the minute they think of something other than the enemy before them. When I raised the camera, though, and it's a stolen camera, not even morally mine, when I pointed it at Philip and dropped the frame around his head and shoulders, he did something I'd never seen: he looked straight into the lens, straight in, as if into the eyes of a lover from whom forgiveness was not yet required or judgement to be feared, and his features *performed*. They swam, the way a dancer loosens his limbs, they composed themselves, and then they waited. It was a quiet flourish, a slow-motion blossoming of skin and muscle. Instead of closing he became porous. See? One elbow rests on the high counter. The strap of the bag pulls his collar askew. His skin is tanned. The day we went out on the river he took his camera (an Instamatic: 'I got it for $3.99 in a junk shop in New York') and lined me up across the table. The beam of his eye passed through the lens, hit me, and bounced off unwelcomed. I felt the skin droop on my skull and the light go out of my face; I felt myself pursing. He lowered the camera without taking a shot and said with a cross laugh, 'You're the worst subject!' 'I know,' I said, and I am. This is no accident. *I* want to be the one doing the looking. I have developed a whole social demeanour with the aim of deflecting attention from my appearance. I actively dislike being looked at. I don't know how so-called *beautiful women* can stand it. 'Looks shouldn't matter,' says Philip without conviction. On another day, in another mood, he says with a vehemence that sounds like anger, 'All this seventies bullshit about there being no such thing as beauty. There's nothing democratic about beauty. Some people are beautiful and that's all there is to it.' You should see the way he speaks to waitresses, and the size of the serves they bring him. I want to say, 'It's all right for *you*,' except that last year I resolved never to become the kind of person who says, 'It's all right for *you*.' 'I understand women,' says Philip. 'I love being looked at.' Maybe that's what beauty is: loving being looked at. The beautiful are greedy. They suck other people's eye-beams into their blood cells and feast on them, growing lovelier and more opulent, while puritans like me who starve themselves for the sake of power diminish daily, wither and shrink till all that's left of them is a hard rail of will. For example. Philip sat down opposite me in the café. 'Look at that,' I whispered. He had already noticed, but was gracious enough to glance up as if surprised. A young woman, a girl, was established alone at a central table. She was dark and smooth, with glossy shins and arms, and dressed in scarlet, white and black—socks, lipstick, ponytail, you know the style, but with that wonderful skin and startling whiteness of eye. Her cup was empty, her chair stood at an angle from the table, her gaze was lost in ether. She sat like a goddess, blind-eyed and motionless, presenting to the world a face innocent of anything that would normally be categorised as expression, but at the same time so outrageously voracious of eye-beams that the café was full of a psychological commotion. I had a terrific urge to laugh, to shout out something—I don't know what; but for the first time in my life I understood why soldiers desecrate shrines. 'Now that,' said Philip with respect, 'is what you would have to call pure.' 'Pure what?' I said. 'Pure being,' he said, then laughed and looked around for the waiter. Is *that* pure being? I thought pure being was when you were alone, when there were no mirrors or shop windows or hubcaps or still pools. Even as I write my story I am aware that I am nowhere near the point of this, that the point recedes from me as I write, that I should be writing about something else. About a man 'half mad with hospitality and thoughts of alcohol'. A club that has no rituals: 'all clubs are sadness clubs,' says its one remaining member, departing. 'The sea that we've all heard so much about.' A dream of death: *'tief und tausendfach zu leben'*. Music, whose 'manifestation is the displacement of air'. It should even be about 'the working class', or a dress 'the colour of hyacinths', or about the battle against sentimentalism: look at the gum tree, see 'the usual mess on the ground'. Once upon a time two women met in a bar. 'I will not talk about the past,' said the furious one. 'But we must,' said the one who burst into tears. Each was afraid that the death of friendship, its murder, would be discovered to be her fault. *I do not give you permission to write about me.* Is there anything cleaner than a clean white shirt? 'This is the hour of lead.' The dirty teeth and lips of red-wine drinkers. The psychological effect of wearing stripes. The punishment of the sick. The punishment for not being beautiful. This is a lifelong thing and begins early. 'No, dear, but you have a face full of character.' And yet perhaps the punishment is for something more serious and obscure than a simple failure to be beautiful. Otherwise why would my lovely, dainty, light-footed…contemporary, my shadow figure Louise, when we were twenty-three, feel the need to press on me the gift of her least flattering hat? Why examine with ostentatious attention the promises on my jar of face cream, then turn on me a blast of her heart-stopping smile and say, *'Poor old thing'*? There was no question in anyone's mind that she was beautiful, I was not. If only I could have been allowed to contemplate her, with frank looks and happy pleasure, as men do—but someone laughs and says, 'I bet you wish you looked like *her*'—so I have to stand beside her, where I can cast only crooked glances, bent ones out of the corner of my eye. *Elle est plus belle que toi.* I know. You are right. She is. But years later, minding her house, I forced the lock on the cupboard under the stairs and found a shoe-box stuffed with photos of her taken (you could tell) by besotted men. She lay sated in lacy disarray, or pouted against a puffing, translucent curtain. I looked, and then I put them back in order, and now I am writing this. Still, we hear of brutal strokes: 'you must remember,' says the famous Greek composer to Charmian Clift on her island, 'that you are no longer young, no longer beautiful'; of clear statements of hierarchy: a man, speechless at the question 'And what does Mrs Calvino do?', replies at last in a reverential tone, 'Mrs Calvino…is a very beautiful woman'; of whipflicks in moving cars: 'And what does your daughter look like? Does she wear ugly ankle socks, like you?' The heart, always eager to be of service, trips over with its tray of china and lies down disconsolate among the pieces. But bow the head, kiss the rod. In humble acceptance stirs the seed of power. Philip read a story I published about him. He made no comment, though he told me later that a woman we both knew had asked him what he was *going to do about it* (I will be obliged to take action, says the woman in the bar) but at one o'clock in the morning (high summer, I'll stick in a moon, some elms on an avenue half a mile away, a hot wind streaming in off the stony rises, sleep not possible) I saw him moving towards me across the bare park, walking slowly in his flapping trousers, trying like me to breathe the hot wind, and I saw immediately that there was no point in greeting him. The grass made a small stiff sound where I put my feet, I did not call out but kept on walking, we passed in silence with our eyes on the ground, and the next time I saw him, in daylight in a street, he said, 'At that moment I would have liked to sink into the ground. I did not want to be part of what you were looking at.' I am writing this in a hotel room. I like the room, I pay for it, for the moment it is mine, but its mirror, some kind of false antique in a heavy frame, is hung on a wall that's at right angles to the table where I work, and whenever I look up from this exercise book I have to see myself getting older, my doubtful expressions and downward lines; so every morning after I have read the paper with scissors in my hand and stuck its manageable stories ('manslaughter, or jealousy, or business, or motor-car racing') into my notebook, I heave the mirror down and stand it on the carpet with its face to the wall. Once I brought my camera here and took some pictures of myself in the mirror. They came out crooked. One side of my head looked higher than the other, and slightly flatter. I couldn't tell whether this was due to the way I had slept on my hair, or whether the lens—or perhaps the mirror itself—contained some distorting property which in waking life, I mean life without camera, was not apparent. Anyway I showed the photos to my friend, a painter, who glanced at them and said with a laugh, handing them back, 'The artist's obligatory self-portrait.' She was only teasing but I was abashed, as if caught out in a naivety. In the afternoons I go out walking (gardens, the bank, shops displaying racks of the ill-made shoes our country produces) and when I return the maids have done the room and hung the mirror back on its hook. I let it be. I even look at myself. Outside my hotel window a tremendous excavation is under way. Early on I thought of taking a series of photos of the progress of the hole, and I did begin it, but now I find it's more fun just to stand at the window with the camera up to my eye and not press the shutter at all, even when the men in hard hats spot me and caper about, rolling their bare shoulders and mugging to make me laugh. I'm just practising looking. The racket from the site is indescribable, and according to law they are not permitted to turn on the gouging machines till seven a.m., but sometimes at night or very early in the morning, before light, someone comes on to the site and shifts things, as if to make a point. Once, at four a.m., I half woke and heard some metal pipes being slung about, but because they were big and hollow, or because I was happy in this room and because nobody knows where I am, I experienced the sound as music: they clashed and chimed with a foreign melody, in a rhythm that was syncopated and full of long pauses, and when the morning came and I woke properly I remembered my dream: that Philip had found me, that he had come to the room and brought me a bunch of grapes which was a work of art. A woman had written a story on the grapes. Each grape bore a single word. I ate each one as I read it, and was so absorbed that I got three-quarters of the way through the bunch before I realised that it had been meant as a present for somebody else, and that perhaps the woman who had written the story on the grapes was me. The people at the hotel are not able to tell me what kind of building is to be erected on the site when the excavation is completed. One day trucks will pour the concrete; the next, workers will walk across it in boots. I'd like to show my photos of the hole to someone. Look— you can see its squared-out sandy bottom scarred by backhoe treads, its yellow and opal walls dripping rust stains, a wooden ladder (feeble as a thought) reaching only

173

halfway out, the floor's six cuboid indentations like escape routes that lead deeper into the rock—but most people prefer photos of other human beings, or of themselves. 'I was a beautiful baby,' says Philip. 'I had all this curly hair, and always a wicked look, turning away.' The photo, when he shows it to me, is of a puddingy baby with oiled locks and a smug expression. There is a story to be written about that photo, but this is not it.

WHAT WE SAY

I WAS KNEELING at the open fridge door, with the cloth in my right hand and the glass shelf balanced on the palm of my left. She came past at a fast clip, wearing my black shoes and pretending I wasn't there. I spoke sharply to her, from my supplicant's posture.

'Death to mother. Death,' she replied, and clapped the gate to behind her.

It had once been a kind of family joke, but I lost the knack of the shelf for a moment and though it didn't break there was quite a bit of blood. After I had cleaned up and put the apron in a bucket to soak, I went to the phone and began to make arrangements.

In Sydney my friend, the old-fashioned sort of friend who works on your visit and wants you to be happy, gave me two tickets to the morning dress rehearsal of *Rigoletto*. I went with Natalie. She knew how to get there and which door to go in. 'At your age, you've never been inside the *Opera* House?' Great things and small forged through the blinding Harbour water. We hurried, we ran.

At the first interval we went outside. A man I knew said, 'I like your shirt. What would you call that colour—hyacinth?' At the second interval we stayed in our seats so we could keep up our conversation which is no more I suppose than exalted gossip but which seems, because of Natalie's oblique perceptions, a most delicate, hilarious and ephemeral tissue of mind.

At lunchtime we dashed, puffy-eyed and red-nosed, into the kitchen of my thoughtful friend. He was standing at the stove, looking up at us over his shoulder and smiling: he likes to teach me things, he likes to see me learning.

'How was it?'

'Fabulous! We cried *buckets*!'

Another man was leaning against the window frame with his arms crossed and his hair standing on end. His skin was pale, as if he had crept out from some burrow where he had lain for a long time in a cramped and twisted position.

'You cried?' he said. 'You mean you actually shed tears?'

Look out, I thought; one of these. I was still having to blow my nose, and was ready to ride rough-shod. My friend put the spaghetti on the table and we all sat down.

'I'm starving,' said Natalie.

'What a plot,' I raved. 'So tight you couldn't stick a pin in it.'

'What was your worst moment?' said Natalie.

'Oh, when he bends over the sack to gloat, and then from offstage comes the Duke's voice, singing his song. The way he freezes, in that bent-over posture, over the sack.'

The sack, in a sack. I had a best friend once, my intellectual companion of ten years, on paper from land to land and then in person: she was the one who first told me the story of *Rigoletto* and I will never forget the way her voice sank to a thread of horror: 'And the murderer gives him his daughter's body on the river-bank, *in a sack*.' A river flows: that is its nature. Its sluggish water can work any discarded object loose from the bank and carry it further, lump it lengthwise, nudge it and roll it and shift it, bear it away and along and out of sight.

'Yes, that was bad all right,' said Natalie, 'but mine was when he realised that his daughter was in the bed-chamber with the Duke.'

We picked up our forks and began to eat. The back door opened on to a narrow concrete yard, but light was bouncing down the grey walls and the air was warm, and as I ate I thought, Why don't I live here? In the sun?

'Also,' I said, 'I *love* what it's about. About the impossibility of shielding your children from the evil of the world.'

There was a pause.

'Well, yes, it is about that,' said my tactful friend, 'but it's also about the greatest fear men have. Which is the fear of losing their daughters. Of losing them to younger men. Into the world of sex.'

We sat at the table quietly eating. Words which people use and pretend to understand floated in silence and bumped among our heads. Virgin. Treasure. Perfect. Clean. My darling. Anima. Soul.

Natalie spoke in her light, courteous voice. 'If that's what it's about,' she said, 'what do you think the women in the audience were responding to?'—for in our bags were two sodden handkerchiefs.

The salad went round.

'I don't know,' said my friend. 'You tell me.'

We said nothing. We looked into our plates.

'That fear men have,' said my friend. 'Literature and art are full of it.'

My skin gave a mutinous prickle.

'*Do* women have a fundamental fear?' said my friend.

Natalie and I glanced at each other and back to the tabletop.

'A fear of violation, maybe?' he said. He got up and filled the kettle. The silence was not a silence but a quietness of thinking. I knew what Natalie was thinking. She was wishing the conversation had not taken this particular turn. I was wishing the same thing. Stumped, struck dumb: failed again, failed to think and talk in that pattern they use. I had nothing to say. Nothing came to my mind that had any bearing on the matter.

Should I say 'But violation is our destiny'? Or should I say '*Nothing can be sole or whole/ That has not been rent*'? But before I could open my mouth, a worst moment came to me: the letter arrives from my best friend on the road in another country: 'He was wearing mirror sunglasses which he did not take off, I tried to plead but I could not speak his language, he tore out handfuls of my hair, he kicked me and pushed me out of the car, I crawled to the river, I could smell the water, it was dirty but I washed myself, a farm girl found me, her family is looking after me, I think I will be all right, please answer, above all, don't tell my father, love.' I got down on my elbows in the yard and put my face into the dirt, I wept, I groaned. That night I went as usual to the lesson. *All I can do is try to make something perfect for you, for your poor body, with my clumsy and ignorant one*: I breathed and moved as the teacher showed us, and she came past me in the class and touched me on the head and said, 'This must mean a lot to you—you are doing it so beautifully.'

'Violation,' said Natalie, as if to gain time.

'It would be necessary,' I said, 'to examine all of women's writing, to see if the fear of violation is the major theme of it.'

'Some feminist theoretician somewhere has probably already done it,' said the stranger who had been surprised that *Rigoletto* could draw tears.

'Barbara Baynton, for instance,' said my friend. 'Have you read that story of hers called *The Chosen Vessel*? The woman knows the man is outside waiting for dark. She puts the brooch on the table. It's the only valuable thing she owns. She puts it there as an offering—to appease him. She wants to buy him off.'

The brooch. The mirror sunglasses. The feeble lock. The weakened wall that gives. What stops these conversations is shame, and grief.

'We don't have a tradition in the way you blokes do,' I said.

Everybody moved and laughed, with relief.

'There must be a line of women's writing,' said Natalie, 'running from the beginning till now.'

'It's a shadow tradition,' I said. 'It's there, but nobody knows what it is.'

'We've been trained in *your* tradition,' said Natalie. 'We're honorary men.'

She was not looking at me, nor I at her.

The coffee was ready, and we drank it. Natalie went to pick up her children from school. My friend put in the plug and began to wash the dishes. The stranger tilted his chair back against the wall, and I leaned on the bench.

'What happened to your hand?' he said.

'I cut it on the glass shelf yesterday,' I said, 'when I was defrosting the fridge.'

'There's a packet of Band-aids in the fruit bowl,' said my friend from the sink.

I stripped off the old plaster and took a fresh one from the dish. But before I could yank its little ripcord and pull it out of its wrapper, the stranger got up from his chair, walked all the way round the table and across the room, and stopped in front of me. He took the Band-aid and said, 'Do you want me to put it on for you?'

I drew a breath to say *what we say*: 'Oh, it's all right, thanks! I can do it myself.'

But instead, I don't know why, I let out my independent breath, and drew another. I gave him my hand.

'Do you like dressing wounds?' I said, in a smart tone to cover my surprise.

He did not answer this, but spread out my palm and had a good look at the cut. It was deep and precise, like a freshly dug trench, bloody still at the bottom, but with nasty white soggy edges where the plaster had prevented the skin from drying.

'You've made a mess of yourself, haven't you,' he said.

'Oh, it's nothing much,' I said airily. 'It only hurt while it was actually happening.'

He was not listening. He was concentrating on the plaster. His fingers were pale, square and clean. He peeled off the two protective flaps and laid the sticky bandage across the cut. He pressed one side of it, and then the other, against my skin, smoothed them flat with his thumbs, and let go.